NO LONGER SCARBOROUGH

STEWART J. CLARK

Copyright © Stewart J Clark – 2023

All rights reserved. No part of this publication may be reproduced, stored in a retrieval system, or transmitted, in any form or by any means, electronic, mechanical, photocopying, recording or otherwise, without the prior permission of the copyright owners and the publisher.

Stewart J Clark asserts his right to be identified as the author of this work in accordance with the Copyright, Designs and Patents Act 1988.

This is a work of fiction. Names, characters, places, and incidents are either the product of the author's imagination or are used fictitiously and any resemblance to actual persons, living or dead, events or locales is entirely coincidental.

ISBN: 979-8-37751-874-7

1

Date: Late Autumn.
Time: Night.
Location: Cliff House, Ravenscar, North Yorkshire.
Weather: Stormy.

The fire has taken everything. Our medical supplies, spare clothes, food, tools, and my old diary, which is why I'm starting from scratch. We might've burned too, had we not heard the lightning strike the roof.

It was brewing all day. The air was thick and damp and the clouds a grey soup, which smudged out the sun and bought about an early nightfall. It hadn't been a problem. In fact, we'd been having a lovely time. Finished off the pasta, then a box of pillow mints, then we spent a good few hours in the games room – pool, table football, darts, dominos, more pool - then CRASH. The sky is lit up like a Christmas tree and the thunder sounded like two angry giants with hacking coughs. But, of course, we've seen worse and been stranded in more vulnerable places, so we continued our games oblivious to the impending threat. It wasn't until an especially loud crack rattled the windows and floorboards, did we throw down our cues and run to investigate.

Brooke was the first to smell the smoke. She turned to me, her eyes lit up with childish excitement, and pointed towards the stairs where the air had turned hazy and grey. Within moments we were coughing and could feel the rising heat. I remembered our supplies were stashed on the third floor, but it was already too late. There was no way I could risk our safety by rushing upstairs to retrieve them, so I grabbed Brooke's arm and we made for the exit.

Outside, the night was alive as blue and yellow forks broke through the clouds, illuminating the North Sea, which was a swirling, foaming mass. The top half of The Ravenhall Hotel was engulfed in fire and swarms of sparks blew in the warm wind and ignited the bushes and grass around us.

"Rendezvous." I yelled, and Brooke stopped grinning and nodded.

We ran down Station Road leaving the red village behind, and cut through a field where I stumbled on a pile of bones - probably a cow - and would've gone over, had Brooke not grabbed the back of my top and steadied me. That was when the rain hit. Great warm rivers which soaked us to the skin.

Our agreed rendezvous point was an old radar station from World War II (now reduced to four concrete shells on a grassy bank, not far from the cliff edge). We ducked into the nearest and paused there to catch our breath. Brooke's exhilaration was over as quickly as it had begun.

"Fucking nature, I swear to god." She pulled off her top and wrung out rivulets of sooty rain. "You alright?"

I told her that I was.

"I was totally winning as well," she said. "I was, wasn't I?"

I barely heard. I was too busy thinking about our tools going up in smoke. She must've read my mind.

"It's fine," she said. "I reckon the rain'll put the fire out."

We waited. The storm went on forever and by the time it had rolled off to the south, the humid air had been replaced by a bitter north-easterly which did nothing to dry our clothes. We trudged back to the centre expecting the worst, and indeed, my pessimism was rewarded. The ground smouldered beneath our shoes and the choking tendrils filled the air like a black fog. The Ravenhall was a glowing pile of rubble, as was much of its surroundings - the undergrowth, the abandoned vehicles, the lodges nearby - and it was still too hot to get up close. Not that we had to. It was plain to see that none of our supplies could've survived. All we had now were the clothes on our backs, and the knives in our belts.

"Screw this," said Brooke turning away. "Need shelter and that."

We'd carried out a full sweep of the village upon arrival, so knew the remaining buildings were clear. We headed upwind and made for Cliff House, an old property, from the 1890s I think. The roof's pretty much intact, as are the windows and doors, and there's no burst pipes and no bodies (human or animal). We managed to jimmy open a small window around the back and climb inside. Such a relief to be out of the elements.

Brooke's asleep on the sofa now, wrapped in a pile of blankets, looking a bit like a caterpillar in a cocoon. I volunteered to take first watch as I knew my monkey mind would never rest after the evening's events. I've hung our damp clothes on an old wooden rack in the kitchen, and also searched through the cupboards and drawers. There's very little in the way of food and drink, just a jar of instant coffee and a tin of pineapples. I *did* find this though, stuck on a high shelf among the cookbooks, and figured I might as well start a new diary.

Enoch Powell once said, "To write a diary is like returning to one's own vomit."

That makes me laugh, but I disagree entirely. Writing always helps.

2

Time: Mid-morning.
Location: Cliff House, Ravenscar.
Weather: The chilly northerly persists, but it's a million times better than yesterday.

"Star?"

After a restless few hours, I woke to find Brooke standing over me, a mug of hot coffee in one hand and a toilet roll in the other. "I dug an extra hole out back if you need to shit."

I wished her a good morning too and went outside to take care of business. Afterwards we sat at the old kitchen table, coffee in hand and the tin of pineapple chunks between us. Brooke grimaced but ate her half without complaining and then pushed the rest towards me. When I opened my mouth to speak, she stopped me.

"Don't."

"I haven't said anything yet."

"And you don't need to." She smiled. "We screwed the pooch – long, hard and without protection. We never should've squeltered in such a massive, unwieldy building. We never should've taken our eyes off the storm. We never should've kept our kit out of reach. But we did. And it's gone and we can't change that. Shit happens. Especially to us." She gulped down half of her coffee. "I get it, alright. We're back in action. Holiday's over, but at least we had a bloody good one."

I couldn't disagree, about our mistakes *or* the 'holiday'. We came here for some much needed respite after miles of travel through the hot, dry summer. Brooke had suggested Ravenscar and I readily agreed because I missed the Yorkshire coast, and I especially missed the sea. Upon arrival, we were surprised to find that the village was completely empty (probably for weeks, possibly for months). Wreckers had not been through either, judging from the intact buildings and the generous amounts of food that remained. We set up camp in The Ravenhall and enjoyed a blissful break, sleeping and eating and reading and playing in the aforementioned games room. Having the run of an entire village was wonderful, but in retrospect the extended period of peace made us too relaxed. Too complacent. And well...Brooke spelled it out accurately enough: shit happened. There's no point dwelling on it now. Learn and move on, or at least try to.

She was leaning back in her chair and almost toppled before catching a hold of the table's edge and righting herself. "So what's the plan, Stan? To go a-hunting and a-gathering? Replace all the stuff we lost?"

I nodded. Through the window I could see the grey sky, the watery autumn sun and the bare trees waving in the chilly wind. "As a matter of priority."

Brooke grabbed her empty mug and tossed it into the sink where it shattered. "So what are we waiting for? It's not like we have bags to pack!"

"We need a map. There isn't one here, I looked last night. Maybe there's one in the tearoom?"

"Sure. We'll scour the place, find what we can before moving out." I must've been staring through the window again, as she knocked lightly on the table. "You with me, Star?"

"I'm fine. I just don't like the thought of travelling so light. Not this late in the year. Not after last time."

Brooke suddenly looked serious – a rare and unnerving sight. "Yeah, don't remind me."

Last winter almost got us. We were in Lancashire at the time, nearing the rural outskirts when a blizzard hit. The worst I've ever seen and ever hope to see. There was no shelter in sight. There *was* no sight unless you count the swirling walls of snow and sleet being carried along by the gale force wind. A total whiteout. It was scary.

We stumbled around for ages, probably going in circles as the snow rose over our shoes and then up to our knees. I've never felt cold like it. It seemed to burn my skin, and penetrate right through to the bone, despite the layers of clothes I had on. Breathing was hard, communication even harder. Thank heavens we spotted the tractor when we did. Just a distant green and black flash at first, it could've been anything, but it looked solid enough. By gripping each other's arms, we manged to reach it, falling against the huge tyre, and finally crowbarring the door and crawling into the cab. Crying with relief as we shut out the elements. It was cramped of course. Just the one seat, and some space on the floor around it. But we didn't care. After that prolonged period of cold and terror, it might as well have been a mansion with a swimming pool, tennis courts and a private library. The blizzard continued to pound at the windows and roof throughout the night and well into the next day, and it was three whole days before we felt safe enough to venture across the snowbanks and seek out a more permanent shelter. Again, we didn't care during those three days; they passed like a dream all things considered. We had a small gas stove for warm drinks, as well as blankets and spare layers of winter clothes. We had books to pass the time and we had containers to gather snow to melt and heat, and we had plenty of tinned food. When it came time to move on, we had a map and a compass to consult, so we could plan our route more carefully than we had done so before.

Sounds so obvious, but without those little things, I doubt we would've survived. We would've frozen solid along with the rest of Lancashire, and not thawed out until the spring. Preparation is everything, and we vowed that we would not be caught out like that again. We'd have all the tools and supplies as well as a safe place to squelter during the worst weeks of winter. If only things were that simple...

"You know what?" Brooke's blue eyes had lit up like yesterday's night sky. "We're only what? Ten miles from home?"

My stomach turned. "No. No, we can't."

"Come on, dude. Desperate times and all that."

"I'd just rather we didn't."

She sighed and nodded. "North then. We could reach Robin Hood's Bay in a couple of hours. And if that's gone to hell, we keep on to Whitby. Visit Dracula's grave while we're at it."

"Hm."

"But come on. Back home we know where things are. Aaaand we know the quickest ways to get to them. I reckon we could be in and out in a day or two, know what I mean?"

I didn't respond. My throat was suddenly parched, like I'd swallowed a sponge.

"Or maybe, *I* could be in and out within a day. We set up a rendezvous on the outskirts and you can wait for me th—"

"You can't go in alone."

"Sure I can. I'm a big girl."

"Too dangerous, Brooke."

"Really?" She sighed again and drummed her blunt nails on the table. "I get why you don't want to go back, I understand. And I don't blame you one little bit after what happened. What *almost* happened. But it was two years ago. It's done, and we've dealt with a lot of crap since then. We're stronger."

"I know. And it's not because of...that."

"So what is it then?"

"It's just...I don't want to."

I ate my share of the pineapple. It tasted like tangy rubber, but at that moment it was easier to focus on that, rather than Brooke.

At last she relented. "Fine. Alright. We don't have to. But we need to think of something, cos there's no guarantee that Hood's or Whitby will be any safer. And I doubt we'll be able to scrounge half of what's needed from the caravans and garden sheds around here." She scraped back her chair and made for the door. "I'll find us a map and that."

While she was gone, I sat in the gloomy silence, my thoughts twisting away. She was right of course, going there would be easier - physically at least. It would be so much quicker than combing through unfamiliar sites. We've done plenty of that, but only when we've had the luxury of time.

There was something else too. It was about more than just convenience for Brooke, I had read it on her face. When she had mentioned *home,* there had been a kind of longing. A deep desire, maybe. I felt nothing of the sort, but I understood, and the more I thought about it, the more lousy I felt for telling her *no.*

I sat and I chewed my lower lip, and I thought of excuses, and I tried to come up with a better plan. And I failed to do either. When Brooke returned at last and placed a map on the table, I had nothing.

"OK," I said. "Scarborough."

3

Time: Near dawn.
Location: Cliff House. Ravenscar.
Weather: Air is still, but cold.

After our rather sad pineapple breakfast, we spent the rest of yesterday gathering what essentials we could (food being the priority). We searched (and re-searched) every building left standing, but there wasn't a lot left. We did find a couple of pretty robust rucksacks as well as some tins still in date, so I suppose it wasn't a total waste of time.

The air is still heavy with smoke from the blackened ruins. It's so gutting to see The Ravenhall in ashes. It was a great building, and one of the original developed here - 1770s I think. Ravenscar is such an interesting place in general. I've always thought so ever since I studied it for my geography coursework. During Roman times there was a signal station - one of a chain dotted along the Yorkshire Coast - which would signal a warning to local communities if there were any approaching enemy ships. After that, there was an alum works, then a brickworks and a railway station. It wasn't always called Ravenscar either. Up until the 1890s it was called Peak, or The Peak. There were big plans for what was just a sleepy village. Developers wanted to make it the next coastal resort like Scarborough and Whitby, and they set about laying roads and putting up houses and even installing sewers and other utilities. But it wasn't to be. Maybe due to the lack of a beach - it's hard to market a place as a seaside resort when instead of sand, there's just 600 feet of cliff onto sharp limestone rocks. Anyway, for whatever reason, the town remained unfinished - but I suppose these days that's not unusual. Everywhere could be considered unfinished.

As if we needed another reminder of the encroaching winter, the sunset came early and the air turned crisp, so we returned to Cliff House to settle in for the night. Dinner consisted of a cup-a-soup, a tin of beans and a tin of hot dog sausages. We played several games of Crazy Eights, all of which I won (though I'm sure Brooke was letting me). She's being extra nice at the moment, even offering take both watches so I could sleep right through. I told her *no*, we both need all the rest we can get.

It's almost dawn. The seaward horizon is starting to glow. I'd be lying if I said it was a welcome sight. In just a few short hours it'll be time to go back.

We're officially out of food. Had the last of it for breakfast – two tins of salmon. Hopefully the Omega-3s will give me an emotional boost. Bloody hell, I need it.

We decided on two possible routes to Scarborough. The first is The Cleveland Way, which is the path that snakes along the top of the cliff, the second is the cinder track – once the old railway line that ran the twenty miles between Scarborough and Whitby (1885 till 1965), stopping at Ravenscar/Peak station along the way. Both are direct, but the cinder track is more likely to be overgrown and flooded, maybe impassable in places. There are also more covered sections where we might be vulnerable to Wreckers or animals.

So, Cleveland Way it is.

I insisted we draw up a shopping list for when we arrive. It ranges from the essential to the useful-if-we-can-find-it and goes as follows:

Medical supplies – Paracetamol, aspirin, ibuprofen (or appropriate painkillers), antihistamines, antibiotics, surgical blades, plasters, bandages. Tweezers.
Spare food (preferably a weeks' worth).
Tin openers.
Spare changes of clothes.
Winter hats and gloves.
A box or two of spare masks.
At least two Swiss Army Knives – must include bottle openers.
Matches (preferably waterproof). Cigarette lighters. Candles.
Toothbrushes and toothpaste.
Tampons.
A screwdriver.
A small hammer.
A Crowbar (if not too heavy and cumbersome).
A sewing kit. (Always useful for short term repairs.)
Two thermos flasks.
Two bottles for water (or a couple of those bladder things. Brooke suggested condoms but I think she was joking).
Compass.
A length of rope.

Torches.
Spare batteries.
Toilet roll. (Most places still have at least one roll, but it's always worth having spares for emergencies.)

  We're leaving in a minute. I feel a bit sick. I've checked my knife holster at least a dozen times. I'm doing my best to be enthusiastic for Brooke's sake. She's acting like its Christmas morning. You'd never believe she's five years older than me!

4

Time: Early afternoon.
Location: Cleveland Way.
Weather: Bright, but strong gusts.

OK, so The Brontë sisters had the Yorkshire Moors, Wordsworth had his Lake District daffodils and Mary Shelley, by some accounts, had her mother's grave. I, Nova Edgecomb, have the sea. Including (but not limited to) the North Sea. I missed it so much while we were inland. Its size, its power, its colour, its ever-changing nature. One minute, it can be as flat as a turquoise mirror and then the next – a swirling, swelling torrent of black lava. I never get bored by it, and today is no exception. Just breathing in the salty, sea-weedy smell and listening to the constant rumble as it scrapes over the pebbles, rocks and sand has lifted my spirits.

Cleveland Way hasn't changed all that much. Obviously, it's far more overgrown and some of the wooden steps have rotted and sunk, but we managed to traverse the steep muddy banks by sliding down on our bums (careful not to tear our jeans). At one point, about a mile or so past Hayburn Wyke, an entire section of cliff had collapsed onto the beach, taking the path with it. We managed to get around by wading through the grassy fields, taking care to not to tread on the sharp cattle bones.

Travel has been extremely slow and cautious, with frequent pauses to watch and listen, and examine the paths and verges for signs of human and animal tracks. It's taken half a day to cover the eight or so miles, but it has paid off. No accidents or near misses, and we've gone unnoticed. We've only seen one lot of people - a group of five - maybe a family. They were below us on the beach gathering driftwood. Probably harmless Ghosts, but we didn't let them see us. We stayed low and hurried on until we were a safe distance away.

Right now, we're taking a quick breather beside the Long Nab Bird Observatory (which is somehow still standing despite being little more than a reinforced shed). From here we can see the castle headland and to the right, the peak of Oliver's Mount. Our first sighting in two years. So familiar, yet so strange. There's no turning back now.

Brooke just noticed me writing. "Another list?" She asked, with a wry smile.

"Not yet."

"Oh, so you're Bridget Jones-ing it again. Can I have a read?"

"Of course not."

"Well, whatever. When you're done gushing over Mr Darcy, or whatever, shall we get going? Bloody starving."

Despite the tightness in my lower gut, I'm getting hungry too. We'll just have to wait until we reach the town. Hopefully there'll be plenty there.

Hopefully it'll be worth it.

5

Time: Night.
Location: High Mill Drive. Burniston Road, Scarborough.
Weather: Still.

The rest of the journey passed without incident, and we reached the outskirts of town as the sun was dipping behind the headland, giving the castle a red halo. We stopped at the top of the steps leading towards Scalby Beck and the North Bay beyond. There was no one in sight, so we took a few minutes to reacquaint ourselves with the view.

The Old Scalby Mills pub remains intact minus its windows, as does The Sea Life Centre (although the once shiny-white pyramids which cover the aquarium are now stained green with weeds and algae). It was high tide and the sea was rough again, slamming against the wall and washing over the promenade, which is now veined with deep fissures and cracks. At some point the railings must've broken free and sunk into the water.

As I stood there, I had a weird feeling like I was a stranger here...or perhaps an invader. Yes, invader would be a more appropriate word. After all, a lot of Scarborough's history concerned invaders in one form or another. Four thousand years ago it was the Bronze Age settlers who built their roundhouses on the headland. Two thousand years back, it was the Romans with their signal station (part of the chain which connected to Ravenscar's). One thousand years, it was the Vikings, which is probably where the town got its name. It comes from Old Norse: Scar meaning 'cliff'. Borough meaning 'village'.

Brooke sucked in a deep breath. "Ah, dead fish and rotting seaweed. Welcome home."

The sun fell out of sight and the sky was darkening by the second. Both of our stomachs were growling, so we opted not to descend the steps but to find a safe place for the night. We trudged west, through more waist-high fields and onto the cracked tarmac that was once Burniston Road. Scarborough Youth Hostel had burned down at some point, so we continued over Scalby Beck and headed up the hill for High Mill Drive, a small cul-de-sac just off the main road. (Possible escape routes include the golf course to the south, or Hillcrest Avenue which leads up to the cinder track.) We selected an intact looking semi, and after the usual checks, climbed inside via the kitchen window.

Thank heavens, there was food. Not a lot, but enough so that we didn't have to venture back outside to look. There was a tin of red kidney beans, a tin of Stagg Chili and a pot noodle. Oh, and I spotted an apple tree in the back garden and managed to pull down half a dozen edible ones. Enough so we'll have a nutritious breakfast tomorrow.

There's not a lot else in here. The rooms are sparsely furnished and most of the cupboards and drawers are empty. The bathroom's pretty grim. A body in the tub. A suicide, we think. Most likely a Nostalgalite. He has been there longer than a year judging from the lack of skin. We found a bread knife on the floor nearby, and from the looks of the crusty blood on the tiles and ceiling, it was used to sever a major artery.

We set up camp in the lounge, using the sofa for a bed, and dismantled the dining room table and built a small fire out the back to cook our food and heat a bucket of water for washing. Afterwards, we quickly extinguished the flames so as not to draw unwanted attention.

With dinner out of the way and all of tomorrow's prep complete, I really begun to feel heavy with mounting dread. I could hardly sit still or concentrate. Reading was out of the question despite a healthy bookcase in the dining room, and I felt too tired to draw or play cards. Brooke noticed of course, and we ended up having a bit of a thing.

"So I was thinking," she said, with a forced casualness that was sooo transparent. "Tomorrow, I really do reckon it'll be safer if I go in alone, know what I mean?"

"We've already talked about this."

"Have we? Well, I have a shit memory, so let's start over."

"Let's not. We have a list. We have a plan. We go together or not at all."

"Hear me out, Star. Six hours, that's all I need. I'll get what I can. I'll be back here and—"

"And what am I supposed to do?"

"I dunno, shop local. Check out the buildings round here. There's bound to be *some* useful bits. And from the looks of it, there's no one in them - alive at least." I opened my mouth to object. "Or don't...if you don't want to. You can stay right here. Pick some more apples. Make a crumble."

"I'm not a 1950s bloody housewife, Brooke."

"So, catch up on your sleep then."

"I don't need sleep."

"Yeah, you do. You've hardly slept since the fire. And when you have, you're moaning – and not in a good way."

"I'm fine."

"Are you? Are you really?"

It went on like that for a while. Me trying to convince her I wasn't losing it, and her adamant that I was. We didn't raise our voices (we never talk above a whisper in built-up areas), but I told her in no uncertain terms that I wasn't prepared to spend tomorrow and maybe the day after with my thumb up my arse, while she's out there doing all the risky jobs.

The rest of the evening was spent in a moody silence at the end of which she flopped onto the sofa and turned away from me. But when she awoke later and came to the window to take over the watch, she gave me a hug and said sorry. And I did too.

Just had a dream. Well, a nightmare. One that'll seem so stupid in the light of day, but not when lying here in the darkness, sticking to the cushions with a cold sweat, my flesh crawling, particularly around the left shoulder - those ugly scars.

Brooke was gone – in the nightmare I mean – and *it* was at the window. A face...more of a skull really, but twisted and stretched and looking weirdly like the castle's keep: split down the middle, crumbling, broken, and with wide empty eyes and a grinning mouth. Teeth the colour of disease. Breath, the reek of stale cologne. Skin, the texture of dry sandstone. It was just there. Silent. Watching. Grinning. It was there for me. It wanted me. Not to kill, not yet. That wouldn't be enough. Not until it had...it wanted to, slowly...to...

Anyway, I awoke before it could get inside the room. I awoke and there was nothing at window except the black of night.

I want to wake Brooke (she shouldn't be sleeping anyway, not when she's on watch) but I'll leave her. I don't want to see that worried look in her eyes, not again. Maybe I should've accepted the offer after all: let her go into town while I check out the properties round here. But I can't, not in a million years. What if she didn't come back? What then? That can't happen. We're a team. We've come too far to change that.

6

I never saw my mother die. I didn't see much of anything for quite a while. I don't remember that much, just feelings mostly. Extreme heat and extreme cold, sometimes both at once. I remember my throat burning as if a family of chainsaws had set up home in there. I remember headaches pulling my skull apart and poking at the soft brain tissue inside.

I remember waking properly. I still felt like I'd fallen off a cliff, but somehow I knew I was over the worst. The curtains were ajar. Beyond, it seemed darker and quieter than before. There was just the wheezing of my own breath and the low ringing in my ears. It was unusual: for a while there had been sirens wailing almost constantly, and the beating of helicopters overhead, but now they were gone. I managed to lift an arm from beneath the covers and reach out for my phone. Blank screen. Dead. As was my reading light. Looking back at the curtains, I realised why it was so black outside: the lampposts, which usually cast a warm orange glow, were off.

I managed to sit up. My pillowcase rose with me. It was stuck to my cheek and took some effort to peel free. A gross mixture of sweat, saliva and snot. Lower down it was far worse. I dragged the duvet off and almost puked. I might've done had my sinus's not been clogged. I'll spare you the details, but let's just say there was a bit of everything. I remember thinking *mum'll kill me when she sees the state of these sheets.*

It took ages to get to the bathroom, but my thirst was more urgent than the aching in my limbs and the throbbing in my head. I pulled the bathroom chord. It clicked, but the darkness remained. When I turned on the cold tap, nothing happened at first, then it hissed and sputtered before a steady stream gushed forth. I drank as if I'd just crossed the Sahara. Too much at first. I choked and bought it back up in stringy globs. I went in slower after that. Taking small sips. Half relieved by the live-giving liquid, and half agonized as it scraped past my tender throat. I felt a little better. I even considered knocking on mum's door to warn her about the power cut, but decided against it. She didn't like to be disturbed, especially at night. So, I returned to my icky bed and fell on top of the covers, quickly dropping back into sleep.

My father died when I was baby, so it was just mum and I. We lived to the south of town, on Filey Road, and that's where I spent the entire lockdown and some of the aftermath. The Stephen Joseph Theatre had closed of course, so my job as an usher was on furlough. Bloody hell, those months were hard. Mum was becoming increasingly difficult. She always liked her conspiracies. Spent ages online, reading all about them - the more local the better. For example, she never believed that the Holbeck Hall Hotel collapse in 1993 was due to erosion. She was convinced it was to hide some evidence of a secret Russian bunker that was located in the basement. According to her, the witnesses who claimed to see large cracks forming on the paths and banks around the hotel were just Russian spies, as were the rest of the geologists and so-called experts. Anyway, when the pandemic spread, she was a million times worse. She talked about very little else. She refused to wear a mask in shops and on buses and would often kick-off when challenged by members of staff. The worse things became, and the tighter the rules, the more gleefully obsessed she got. "It's the toilet roll companies," she told me one day, as she sat at the kitchen table painting her new placard. "I guarantee it, Nova dear. You've seen how everyone is stocking up, clearing all the shelves. It's no coincidence."

I stayed in my room as much as I could, only leaving for meals and the bathroom and occasionally to watch TV (I wasn't allowed one in my room) or borrow a book...OK, that's not quite true. I admit that a few times I snuck out my window to go and meet Matthew, who lived across the road. He was my age, give or take a few months. He wasn't my boyfriend exactly, Mum would never have allowed that, but we would hang out at his house and play Xbox and watch Netflix. And sometimes we did it, usually in the small, wooded area at the bottom of Sea View Park or, on one occasion, in an old pillbox on Cayton Bay. (Brooke doesn't believe that, by the way. She's convinced I'm still a virgin!)

By this point, mum had started attending the anti-lockdown protests. Travelling all over the country to join up with 'like-minded folk' to march through the streets waving banners and chanting at anyone who would listen. She'd come home all elated and immediately jump onto her iPad to find out where and when the next one was. She was supposed to be teaching remotely (English literature at Scalby School), but she never did. "What's the point in teaching imaginary fiction, when we're living through a real fiction."

In the week when the Code Red was announced and everyone was warned to remain indoors no matter what, she rushed out to that massive protest in the town centre. I watched a bit of it on Facebook Live. Never seen the place so packed. People had driven in from miles around and crammed together on Westborough to march down to the South Bay.

The following day she was sniffing and trying to mask the occasional cough. The day after, she was talking like she'd smoked ten cigars in a row and swallowed a beaker of sulphuric acid. The day after that, she didn't get out of bed and told me to keep on top of the washing, ironing and hoovering. "It's just a twenty-four hour bug, Nova dear," she croaked, when I offered to call Dr Finn. "Don't get drawn into their lies. I'll be fine in the morning."

She wasn't. And neither was I. I could hardly move, my joints were like rusted iron and my lungs all thick and gluey. It was like the flu only worse. I could just about make it to the kitchen for water and food, but that was about it. Housework was out of the question. I kept expecting her to start calling for me, but she didn't. There was very little noise from her room beside the occasionally scratchy cough.

The day after that, I was too weak to get up. Like I said, I don't exactly know how long I lay there, it's all just a blur (apart from my aforenoted headaches and that messy trip to the bathroom). Could've been days, could've been weeks, I just don't know, and I never will.

And, I'll probably never know how I came through all that, while so many others didn't. Something in my immune system perhaps? Maybe just a bit of luck – good or bad, it's not for me to say. All I know is, I recovered enough to be out of bed for more than a few minutes without collapsing. And I could breathe without wheezing, and drink water without my throat wanting to spontaneously combust. It was then that I became aware of the state of things.

There was no reply when I knocked on her door. I suspected she was dead by then, but it wasn't a fact my mind was able to accept. I called out to her, my voice, though feeble and croaky, was like an airhorn in the silent hallway. Still nothing. I broke the cardinal rule and entered the room without permission. The walls were black with flies, as were the bedsheets and the two placards which she'd placed against the wardrobe (SCAM-DEMIC and

FREEDOM NOT FEAR). Samara Edgecomb was still in bed. A dent under the covers. Motionless. I called her for the last time, just to be certain, and then I backed out into the hall and shut the door. My first thought was to ring for an ambulance, but of course, the phones were forever cut off. *All* the power stayed off, so for a while I just sat on the living room sofa, looking at the blank TV. I don't remember crying, I just remember feeling heavy and numb, like my insides had turned to plasticine.

There was still water in the taps, but within a couple of days it had turned brown, slowed to a trickle and then to a drip, and then nothing. I ate the food from the fridge (tasting none of it) then moved onto the tins and cartons in the cupboards. I didn't return to my own bed. I slept on the sofa. I slept a lot. When I was awake, and not looking at the telly, I spent a lot of time at the windows. There was nothing. No cars on the road, no planes in the sky, no passers-by, not even any movement from Matthew's house, or any of his neighbours. Out the back, the park was equally desolate. No kids on the swings or climbing frames, no parents, no dog walkers. *They're still in lockdown like me*, that's what I told myself.

I'd lost track of time. There was no way to tell the day of the week or the date of the month. The clock above the mantlepiece in the living room continued to tick thanks to its single AA battery, but knowing the hour didn't feel particularly relevant. It still doesn't, though I do occasionally wonder if there *is* anyone out there who knows the actual time and date, you know, if they diligently kept a wind-up clock or watch going, or had enough spare batteries to keep one powered up. Would it make any different though? I'm not sure it would. It's not like there are appointments to keep or jobs to be on time for, and even if there were, there are other, more primitive ways to keep track: the position of the sun or stars for instance, or the shadows on the ground. It's just weird to think that I'm not even certain of how old I am anymore. I must be twenty by now, but I'm not positive.

Anyway, food and drink ran out, but worse than that, my taste and smell was returning. Every time I crossed the hallway, the hot, putrid smell of decay hit the back of my throat. Sometimes at night, I heard scratching on the inside of her door. Sounded a bit like she'd crawled from her bed and was scraping persistently at the wood, though I knew that was impossible. Had to be insects. Or had rats somehow burrowed inside? Lockdown or not, I had to go outside. I threw on a mask (the one I'd kept hidden from mum for fear that she would chuck it onto the fire) and ventured out.

Matthew hurt. The first tangible emotion I'd felt in a while, and it cut right through my heart. I didn't go into his house, but there were enough black insects crawling over the windows to tell me his fate, and that of his family. I knocked of course, knocked for ages and I yelled through the letterbox, but I just got silence in return. That's what I remember most when I stepped outside on that cool, overcast afternoon. The silence. I'd never acknowledged how loud things used to be, even in a relatively small town like this. Now there was nothing. No music, no engines, no voices, no barking, no hammering, drilling, hooting, crashing, slamming. Even the birds and animals seemed to have lost their voices (though they would return in time). I went to Henry Teal's house next door, and then to Mrs O'Hara's further up. If any of them *were* alive, they didn't answer the door or come to the windows.

Back home, the smell was overwhelming. Every in-breath made me want to gag. I thought about gathering her up in the covers and burying her in the back garden, but I just couldn't face it. I wanted to be away from this house. Far away. And I had to know what was happening in the rest of Scarborough. The rest of the world. There had to be help somewhere. I grabbed my work bag instinctively packing my dead phone, house keys and purse, then I secured my mask, and made the journey up Filey Road towards the town centre. The mile and a half walk seemed to go on interminably. Everything was present and correct just...empty. I did wonder if I'd actually died from the virus and was now walking through some sort of purgatory. I paused in Ramshill and thought about heading up Westbourne Grove to call for Jenny. We hadn't really spoken that last year (just the odd message on Facebook) but maybe, just maybe she'd survived. I turned away and continued, putting her out of my thoughts. Mum, Matthew and the neighbours were enough to deal with for now. I crossed Valley Bridge and reached the centre. Masks were scattered everywhere, blowing about in the wind, and I passed a bin that was writhing with rats and maggots. There were people here. Not many, kind of like an early Sunday in midwinter. They were ambling around slowly, taking wide circles around each other. They were dazed, wide eyed, and a few of them were carrying shopping bags. No one spoke. No one even acknowledged anyone else. I avoided them all, walking down the middle of the empty road until I reached Westborough. I'd naively hoped there might be tents set up with tables of food and drink and medics treating the old and sick. Perhaps even a space put aside for people to sleep. A Safe zone, like you get in zombie stories, where the protagonists escape to in the final act, and you know everything's going to be alright. But there was no safe zone. There was nothing beyond the scattering of lost survivors or the empty shops or the scurrying rodents. It might've looked the same, but this was no longer Scarborough.

7

Time: Late evening.
Location: Thornville Avenue, off Burniston Road.
Weather: Gusty and cold now the sun's down.

Medical supplies – Paracetamol, aspirin, ibuprofen, antihistamines, antibiotics, surgical blades, plasters, bandages.
Tweezers.
Spare food.
~~Tin openers.~~
~~Spare changes of clothes.~~
~~Winter hats and gloves.~~
~~Spare masks.~~
At least two Swiss Army Knives – must include bottle openers.
Matches (preferably waterproof). Cigarette lighters. ~~Candles.~~
Toothbrushes and ~~toothpaste~~.
~~Tampons.~~
~~A hammer.~~
~~A screwdriver.~~
Crowbar.
~~A sewing kit.~~
Two thermos flasks.
Two flasks for water.
Compass.
~~A length of rope.~~
Torches.
Spare batteries.
~~Toilet roll.~~

  To quote Judy Garland in The Wizard of Oz, "There's no place like home." To quote Brooke Barden from earlier this evening, "What a fuck-awful pisser of a day."
  OK, so we managed to find a few useful items but not nearly as much as we'd have hoped. Especially concerning the medical supplies. They're the priority and yet they're what proved to be the most elusive. Not a single First Aid kit, not a single bloody pill. Where has it all gone?
  And in addition to that, we had to contend with all the damage and defacement, and finally, to top it all off like a razor-bladed cherry on a poisoned cake, the gruesome discovery this afternoon.

We set off just after sunrise, neither of us having had much sleep. The first unexpected sight was ready to greet us at the top of the hill. The petrol station was ruined. The main building was little more than a shell. All the pumps had been ripped from the ground and it appeared that the concrete beneath had been drilled through and the petrol and diesel tanks had been syphoned. Every last drop.

"Someone was thirsty," whispered Brooke.

"I doubt they took it for vehicles, given the state of the roads. Maybe they've got generators?"

"That's a lot of generators."

We left the main road and continued through the golf course, now a meadow of yellowing grass, swaying in the wind. From there we stuck to gardens and back alleys - places we could duck for cover if anyone or anything worried us. It's pretty great that no matter how well you think you know a place, there's often a shortcut or a narrow lane or a hidden snicket to find. Somewhere new and unexplored. They're easier to discover on foot, especially when travelling at the slow, cautious pace that we were.

My spirits were actually starting to lift. This wasn't so bad. The sea air was the freshest I'd ever known, the distant call of seagulls was pleasantly familiar, plus Brooke's initial excitement was infectious. Last night's dreams were fading into the background, and I was beginning to think that my worries had been needless. But then we got to Cross Lane Hospital and found nothing. And I mean NOTHING. The pharmacy had been picked clean, as if by crows. The cabinets were empty, the food cupboards bare, along with the patient and staff rooms. We snuck through the entire building with growing disbelief and frustration. In the end, we managed to grab a couple of loo rolls and a tin opener, but that was about it.

And it only got worse from there.

We crossed over to Newlands Park Drive and made for the shops. What a mess. The Co-op, the bakery, the greengrocers, the chippy – what hadn't been taken, had been broken. No, not just broken but ripped apart, shattered, stomped on, chewed and spat out, defecated over. Every window had been smashed, every door kicked in, shelves had been ripped out and thrown around, giant penises, labia and juvenile swearwords had been graffitied over the walls in luminous pinks and greens. We found similar scenes at the pub across the road, and then at Northstead Pharmacy and the shops next to that.

We've seen examples of this before of course – Wreckers didn't get their name by accident – but never on this scale. People usually take what they need to live off and then move on. They might break through a door or a window or a roof if it's the only way to gain access. Maybe they'll snap locks with hammers or crow bars, they might even cut through the door of a safe if there's the promise of treasure that can be traded. But in most cases, they'll maintain a certain amount of restraint and respect for the property they've entered. Especially if it was someone's home or small business, and even more so if it's their final resting place. No respect had been shown here. No restraint. It was just wanton destruction for entertainment's sake, and there was very little we could salvage from among the heaps of debris.

We paused for a lunch break behind some bushes on Lowdale Avenue, moodily munching on our remaining apples. Brooke was unusually quiet. She hadn't even commented on the spray-painted genitals. Not so much as a snigger. "I doubt they're still here," she said quietly, as we were preparing to set off again.

"Who?"

"The dirty bastards that did all that. Probably just passing through, right?"

"Yeah, probably."

We headed down Northstead Manor Drive and at the risk of becoming repetitive, much of that was a wreck too. Houses, flats, B&Bs, all pillaged and vandalised. We found a few toiletries here and there, but that was all. Time was getting on. The shadows were lengthening and the gusts of wind growing in strength. It was clear that we would have to continue our search tomorrow, deeper into town. The idea of which did nothing to improve my mood. But that was nothing compared to what followed.

"What about Alpamare?" said Brooke. "Probably gone to shit too, but worth a look. You reckon?"

I agreed. I was pretty familiar with the waterpark. A group of us visited on Jenny's fourteenth birthday. (I told mum it was field trip for School as she never would've allowed me to wear a swimming costume in public, not even a one-piece.)

The Tunny Catch and the Premiere Inn were badly vandalised, so we didn't risk going near either of those. Alpamare looked much better, on the outside at least. The massive front windows were unbroken, as were the jumble of water shoots which snake into the side of the yellow tower.

Inside it was a different story. The smell was overwhelming. The tang of chlorine and suncream had been replaced by a mixture of rotting meat and blocked drains. The foot or so of water which remained in the four pools had turned to a greeny, brown sludge, and there was black mould growing over the walls and windows. The lockers were all flapping open and empty, and the small gift shop had been trashed. It was in the cafe out the back where we found the body.

We've seen a lot of death, but it's usually from sickness, or suicide, or an accident. Neither of us had ever witnessed anything like this. It...he was naked. Nailed to the wall behind the counter. It was hard to tell how long he'd been up there, but he was still decomposing. His jaw was gaping so wide that the bones had most likely broken. His mouth was stuffed full: chocolate bars still in their packets, sauce sachets, sugar lumps, shoved all the way in (and probably down his throat and into his stomach and lungs too). His eyeballs had been removed and placed in the tip jar on the countertop. The empty sockets were crammed full of ten and twenty-pound notes. Someone had smeared a speech bubble on the tiles next to his screaming mouth. "HANDS OFF!" it said. (I'm pretty sure they'd used his blood to write it.)

Without thinking, I'd drawn my knife and I quickly circled the room to make sure no one was lurking under the tables or behind the displays. Unlike Brooke, I didn't go up behind the counter. If I got too close, I knew I would pass out.

"What the fuck *is* this?" she said, staring in sickened fascination towards the victim's groin. "They've even stuck a cocktail umbrella up his dickhole."

"Thanks Detective," I turned away and bit my tongue, willing my stomach contents to stay put, then focused my attention back on the room.

There was a reclining chair and a bundle of towels against the opposite wall, and surrounding that, a few empty tins and wrappers. He'd obviously been squeltering here before the Wrecker (or Wreckers) had come for him.

"I reckon," said Brooke, "someone tried to nick his stash, and he fought back. So they did this. Has to be the same arseholes who trashed everywhere else. Sicko's, I swear to god."

It was almost dark now, and we still didn't have any torches or candles. I felt like we were being watched from every shadowy corner.

"Can we go?" I said, rather pathetically.

"Gladly." Brooke leapfrogged over the counter. "There's nothing left here anyway. Apart from the stuff on this poor sod. And I'm not digging that out."

We left through the fire door and snuck out into the car park, where we took cover behind a rusted ice cream van, and sucked in the sweet, sweet air, hoping to expel the taste of murder from our noses and our minds.

Brooke turned to me. "Are you—"

"I'm fine."

"Puke if you have to. I won't blame you."

"I said, I'm fine."

She gave my shoulder a gentle squeeze. "Remember Center Parcs?"

Despite everything I had to nod and laugh. It was last spring. We were hiking through Sherwood Forest and decided to sneak into the village for a supply run. We ended up in the massive dome and found that the pool had been drained. Despite my initial reservations, Brooke insisted we make a landing pad at the bottom of the dry shoots using seat covers, and then go for a ride - fully clothed obviously! We ended up sliding down for several hours, and after that we rode bikes through the pine scented forest and over to the leisure centre to play table tennis and air hockey and archery. (Although we found that bowling was no fun when you have to manually pick up the pins after every go!) We stayed there a few days in the end. It was a good memory.

It helped.

"Come on," I said, and we made our way out the car park and back onto Burniston Road. "Enough for today."

"Couldn't agree more," said Brooke. "And if you don't wanna stay—"

"One more day, alright? If it's more of the same, then we move on."

"Sounds like a plan."

"Let's get somewhere close." I glanced back at the waterpark. "But not too close."

We found a house on Thornville Avenue - another out of the way cul-de-sac that thankfully looked untouched. We refrained from lighting a fire, so dinner was a tin of cold baked beans, some sweetcorn and a chunk of corned beef. On a happier note, we did find three advent calendars stashed at the back of the cupboard under the stairs. We used the chocolate for poker chips. Brooke won the lot, but she graciously split the pile and we wolfed them down like children!

We set up camp in the spare bedroom, barricading the door with a chest of drawers, and using the rope I found in the shed on Lowdale, I made us an escape route: attaching one end to the leg of the bed and leaving the other by the window.

The sky has cleared at last. The canvas of stars are so bright, and earlier I saw a flash, followed by speck of fire that left an orangey, blue trail. Probably a falling satellite. They're quite common at the moment.

So, one more day here and then we're gone. I honestly can't wait.

8

In the weeks after leaving my house, I spent some time categorising the last of us that remained. I came up with four main types of survivors: Darwinners, Ghosts, Nostalgalites and Wreckers.

Darwinners are what we all aspire to. They've adapted to this new world order and have found ways not only to survive, but to value their time. And to enjoy what they can.

Ghosts like to keep a low profile at all times. If they have to leave their dwellings, they do so unnoticed and leave little trace. They're often alone, but if not, they only keep a few likeminded people around. They survive, but I wouldn't say they are living.

Nostalgalites are the opposite to Darwinners. They can't accept what's happened and cling desperately to their old lives before the pandemic. Obviously, that rarely works out and tragically, their life expectancies are fairly short.

Finally, there's the Wreckers who should be avoided at all costs. They thrive in a world without law and order and take pleasure in breaking the taboo's that were once imposed on them by society. Whether it's in the destruction of their surroundings or of themselves, there are no depths to which they won't sink.

When I first met Brooke, I was undoubtedly a Ghost while she, I'm sorry to say, was a Wrecker.

As I said before, time was no longer a thing but at a guess I'd say it had been between a month to six weeks since I made the short but endless journey from Filey Road into town. I was still waiting. The idea of emergency services swooping in from the outside world was still a possibility. This was all just temporary. Soon the lockdown would end and the quarantine would lift, and we'd all have a chance to bury our dead, and then slowly but surely things would return to normal. Life would pick up where it had left off. I'd go to university to do that history degree, and maybe a PhD, then get a job as a teacher or lecturer. Buy a house, buy a car, fall in love...Yeah, I actually believed all that!

I'd been squeltering in the Stephen Joseph Theatre for a while. I had a small camp set up in the staffroom. Slept on a sofa and kept all my supplies organised in the lockers. I knew the place well enough because I'd ushered there for the best part of three years, but it could still be creepy at night. It's an old building, originally designed as an Odeon Cinema in the mid-30s until it closed in 1988. Alan Ayckbourn converted it into the new SJT in the 90s but kept many of the art deco stylings. Cool during the day, but at night...

So far, no one else had ventured inside. There were often survivors around the town centre, but they were more interested in the cafes, supermarkets, Market Hall and anywhere else with food. Back then there was still fresh (or freshish) supplies available: cakes, biscuits, crackers, dried fruit, crisps, juices, non-dairy milk, that kind of thing. Shop doors hung open so people could wander inside and take what they needed before heading home. It was all so weirdly civilised. Even so, I avoided everyone. I would crouch by the huge, curved window on the theatre's first floor waiting for Northway and Westborough to be completely deserted before sticking on a mask and gloves and sneaking out. I'd always have a list and a route worked out beforehand, so I was never away for long.

I was in the newsagents on Aberdeen Walk gathering bottles of spring water, when I was alerted to the sound of shattering glass in the street outside, followed by a woman singing loudly. Too loudly. I immediately ducked behind the counter and cautiously peered over. She looked to be her mid-twenties. Her dark brown hair hung in lank curtains. She wore grubby jeans which were riding low (and did little to hide the red thong poking up) and a T-shirt with 'Bullshit' printed on the back. I also noticed a tattoo of a cartoon fox on her upper right arm. She had emerged from Florio's, clutching an armful of the house red, some of which had already fallen from her grip and shattered on the pavement, leaving a glassy red stream. Judging from her weaving walk and tone-deaf rendition of I Me Mine, she had enjoyed several bottles already. I waited for her to pass by, only she didn't. She slumped down on the kerb directly opposite, twisted off a lid and drank half the contents in several huge gulps. I watched, fascinated, disgusted. I mean sure, I'd had binges. On one occasion I'd eaten three chocolate brownies off the display in Bonnets – one after the other and not the small ones either - but this was something else. She was drinking like she wanted to die.

I returned to the job at hand, stashing the spring water into my backpack. Once more, I was distracted by a noise outside. Not a bottle this time, nor singing, but a growl and a bark. A Golden

Retriever had emerged from a side street and was sniffing at the spilled wine, following the trail, and closing in slowly on the woman. It was skinny, its fur matted, and its tail was not wagging. It drew closer, reaching her. Sniffed her back, her arm, her shoulder, her hair. It circled slowly, saliva dripping from its jaws.

She noticed it at last. "Hey doggy." She waved a clumsy hand towards its face. It snapped at her fingers. "Hey!" She swung her arm catching it across the tip of its nose and it recoiled, just for a second, before lunging and grasping her by the leg, sinking in its teeth. She let out a cry and flailed both arms, trying to push it away, and the remaining bottles fell and clanked into the road. The dog took several hits but didn't back off this time. The poor thing was wild with hunger. It pulled hard, and woman slumped onto her side and was dragged several feet down the path. "Gerroff,"

My first instinct was to leave her. It was her fault. She was foolish enough to drink herself into oblivion and make herself vulnerable. I dismissed that thought quickly. I was having enough bad dreams, without having another one to add to them. I rushed outside.

"STOP." It didn't stop, just kept on tugging. "LET GO."

The woman was on her front, scratching at the tarmac, failing to get a grip. I was still clutching a bottle of water in each hand. I hurled them both. The first missed completely, and the second bounced uselessly off its back. It didn't notice, or didn't care, it just continued its attack. I then heard the sound of tearing and wondered if it was the material of her jeans, or the flesh of her calf. That spurred me into action. I circled around, approaching the animal from behind and grabbed at its collar with both hands, dragging it back towards me. It began thrashing wildly but didn't let go. It was so strong, considering its state, and the heat from the scrawny body was palpable. With my right hand I reached round to grab its neck and squeezed the lumpy gristle. It gagged, and chocked, finally releasing the woman's leg, but now it was trying to turn towards me, snapping its dripping teeth. I managed to get astride it and close my knees tightly around the hind quarters, pinning it in place, then I increased the pressure on its neck. It snarled and barked and gnashed its jaws. I kept squeezing until its air supply was depleted, and its struggles had finally weakened, and its growls had become a shallow panting. I released my grip and stumbled back, and it took off, limping up Castle Road without looking back.

"Oh. My. God," slurred the woman. "Did you shee that? Shtoopid dog."

The leg of her jeans was tattered and soaked in blood. She was trying to get up, but only succeeded in falling into the gutter among her discarded bottles. For some reason this made her laugh uncontrollably. I wiped my sweating hands down my top and approached.

"You're hurt." My voice was all scratchy. It had been weeks since I'd spoken to anyone. "Do I have your consent to treat you?"

She squinted up at me. "Wot?"

I read about that in one of the manuals, and it must've stuck. Get their consent if you can. That way you avoid a lawsuit down the line.

"I'm a first aider," I said slowly. "I can help if you let me. Your leg's injured."

"Ish not." She glanced down. "Oh, ssshit. Thatsh red."

I helped her up, into the newsagents and through to the backroom where I placed her in a chair by the sink.

"What's your name?" She looked even more confused. "Can you count to ten?"

She grinned. I could smell the wine on her breath. "Fuck off! This isn't shhschool."

"Fine." I turned and made for the door. "Good luck then."

"Brooke. Ish Brooke. Erm, Barden." And she successfully counted to ten.

I hesitated in the doorway. Her trail of blood ran all the way though the shop and was now pooling at her feet. She was in no state to deal with it, or with the infection that might follow. That wasn't my fault though...

"Husband's dead," she muttered. "They're all dead."

"Just keep still." I grabbed the first aid kit from my bag and a pair of scissors from a mug on the table and set about cutting the jeans free from the wound. It looked worse than it was. The skin was torn in several places, but would not require stitches. I set about cleaning it while she swayed back and forth on the chair. Several times I had to steady her before she could topple on the tiles.

"Whosh are you?" she asked, as I applied the dressing and wound it tight.

"Nova." I said. "Nova Edgecomb."

She grinned again. Her teeth were stained red. "Nova!"

"It means star."

"So why aren't you called *star*?"

"Same reason you're not called *body of water*."

Brooke guffawed. "Thassh pretty right, actually. I so need to pissh."

"You'll have to control yourself until I'm finished."

"Yesh momma."

I finished bandaging her up and to my disbelief she immediately lurched out of her chair, hiked down her jeans and thong, and climbed up onto the sideboard, where she relieved herself into the sink, almost falling in several times. She used the dishcloth to wipe herself then buttoned up and dropped back into the chair. "Thatsh better."

I was more than ready leave by now, so I reached into my bag, found the right box of pills and handed them over.

"Whash this?"

I explained they were Amoxicillin - a type of Penicillin that would kill any bacteria in the wound. "Take three a day. Morning, noon and before going to sleep...without alcohol."

"Wheresh the fun in that?"

"I'll give you some spare bandages, change them three times a week. More often if you get them wet or dirty."

"You a doctor?"

I shook my head. "Just prepared. Got most of these from Boots. Also got some books from the library. It's not like I can call an ambulance. Not at the moment."

She shrugged. "You're like, well shmart."

"And I understand how much pain you're in, Brooke, but alcohol won't help in the long run. It'll just make you more depressed."

"What pain?" she raised her leg. "This isn't sho bad."

"Your husband? You said he died."

"Oh yeah." A third grin, and a chuckle. "I was celebrating, and that."

"Celebrating?"

"Mark was a dick. Like a real dick."

"OK." I packed the first aid kit away and sanitised my hands.

"You leaving me?"

"Want to get back before it's dark."

"Back where?"

I declined to answer.

"Where you from?"

"Here."
"What, the shop? Do you come free with a magazine?"
"Here, as in Scarborough."
"Yeah, I shnow that, but where are you from originally?"
"Scarborough."
"But..." she pointed a shuddering finger towards my dark skin.
"My grandparents were from Nassau."
"NASA? Like the moon?"
"Bahamas."
Slow understanding dawned on her face. "Right, yeah, I shee. Oh, no I'm not racist, I swear. One of my closest slaves is black." She chuckled, then grimaced with realisation. "Soz. That was one of Mark'ssh. Told you he was a dick."
I slung the rucksack around my shoulders and stepped towards the exit.
"You'll be alright, Brooke. Take the pills, change the bandages, drink lots of water. Oh, and beware of the dogs. They're getting hungry."
"No sshit."
"It'll be OK. I'm pretty sure help will arrive soon."
She sat up so quickly the chair almost slid from under her. "Help? Says who?"
"No one, I just think the army or the National Guard or—"
"Batman or James bloody Bond?"
"Don't be stupid."
"You're the one being stoopid if you think help is coming."
"How would *you* know?"
"Cossh, I trudged halfway across the country, that's how. Your angels of mercy are either dead or doing the same thing as the rest of us."
"Oh."
"Scarborough's not the only place that's gone to shit, you know. The whole of England went with it. Probably the whole wide world."
I knew this already, in the back of my mind, but to hear it spelled out, even in a rant by a drunken chav was like taking a sledgehammer to the gut.
"Where've you been the last...however fucking long?"
"Lockdown." I said. "Then I got really ill."
She recoiled and slapped a hand over her mouth and nose. "Sick?"
"I'm better now."

"Good." She relaxed again. "Cos this hangover's gonna be a bitch, and the leg. And I don't need any other shit to add to it."
"You've been outside Scarborough then?"
"Well duh."
"Where?"
"New Hall in Flockton."
"Where?"
"West Yorkshire. And that was a proper lockdown, know what I mean?"
"No."
"It's a prison."
I must've looked surprised or nervous because she laughed some more. "Chill. I never killed anyone. As much as I would've liked to."
"So what happened?"
She yawned. I got a glimpse of her tonsils. "I got busted."
"No, I mean, with the pandemic?"
"I dunno really. In the days before everyone started dropping, there was some talk on the telly about a new variant. Rumours and stuff. Don't think it had a name yet."
"I remember that. They told everyone to stay indoors. Like, no matter what."
"Yeah, but it was already too late by then. Clearly!" She motioned towards the empty street outside. "I reckon it had been here for ages and spread like butter. Through all the shops, hospitals, among those protesters, through the prisons. It killed everyone on my block. Not me though. Must be some kind of immunity, cos, despite all appearances, I'm not that fucking healthy, know what I mean?"
"So you were trapped there. How did you get out?"
"It's hardly San Quentin. I climbed through a window and jumped the fence." She yawned again and once more I was treated to a wave of wine fumes. "Bottom line is…out there it's much like here. Lots and lots of bodies. A few alive people." She glanced down at her wrist where there was no watch. "Oh…so yep. Lots and a few. That's how it is."
"You're certain? A hundred percent?"
"No help coming. Soz." Her eyelids were drooping, and she was starting to slump down in the chair. "Bloody knackered, I swear." She yawned a third time. "You haven't asked?"
"Asked what?"
"What I did."

"I don't think it's relevant. Not anymore."

She chuckled, then her head lolled, and she was lightly snoring. I lifted her from the chair, placed her on the tiles and rolled her into the recovery position. If she were to bring anything up in her sleep, at least she wouldn't drown. I took a final sweep of the building to ensure it was secure for the night, and made my way out.

Brooke Barden. I hoped to goodness I would never have to see her again.

I sat in the dark of The Round staring upon the bare stage. Since 1955 the Theatre in the Round – the first of its kind in Britain - had been performing almost nonstop. Stephen Joseph founded the company in the Scarborough Library, then moved it to Westwood in the 70s, and then finally it came here. A permanent spot. A final resting place. I thought about all those years, all those productions and all those audiences, all the actors, crew, and my colleagues who worked here. Now there was just me, surrounded by 400 empty chairs. Chairs that would mostly likely remain empty, in the shadows where the lights had dimmed, and the last curtain had fallen.

The show was over.

9

Time: Early afternoon.
Location: Graham School, Woodlands Drive.
Weather: Bloody wind. Bloody hail.

Medical supplies – ~~Paracetamol~~, aspirin, ~~ibuprofen~~, antihistamines, antibiotics, surgical blades, ~~plasters~~, bandages.
Tweezers.
Spare food.
~~Tin openers.~~
~~Spare changes of clothes.~~
~~Winter hats and gloves.~~
~~Spare masks.~~
Two Swiss Army Knives with bottle openers.
Matches. ~~Cigarette lighters. Candles.~~
Toothbrushes and ~~toothpaste~~.
~~Tampons.~~
~~A hammer~~
~~A screwdriver.~~
Crowbar.
~~A sewing kit.~~
Two thermos flasks.
Two flasks for water.
~~Compass.~~
~~A length of rope.~~
~~Torches.~~
~~Spare batteries.~~
~~Toilet roll.~~

It was another long night of fitful sleep and an early start at dawn. Our main priority was to investigate Scarborough Hospital. Only a two mile hike, but it took most of the morning as we were being even more careful now. The murder of the *"HANDS OFF"* man was still very much playing on our minds, and we had no intention of being displayed alongside him. We cut through Peasholm Park, circling the lake where I used to love watching the Naval Warfare re-enactments with the miniature WWII ships and planes. The cafe and kiosks had been raided, and the bandstand on the water had capsized, but the island with the Japanese style Pagoda and gardens looked relatively undisturbed.

We headed up The Glen, which connects Peasholm with the Dean Road & Manor Road Cemetery. It's more of a jungle now, and at several points we had to draw our knives and hack through the thick undergrowth. Further up, beneath Glen Bridge, we had to scramble over a huge birch tree that had fallen across the path. We managed it with just a few scratches and dirtied jeans, and from there we took Woodlands Ravine, then crossed Scalby Road and turned up Woodlands Drive.

Our expectations were lower than the sandy bottom of the North Sea, so the sight of Scarborough Hospital as a massive pile of black rubble (as frustrating as it was) did not devastate us as much as it might have. We explored the carpark which was absolutely jampacked (with more vehicles spilling out of the entrance and along the roads, pavements and verges). Bloody hell, those last few days here, it doesn't bear thinking about. There were corpses sat upright behind the steering wheels, staring blankly out the windscreens. More lay curled up on the backseats, and there were at least twenty others lying in the long grass, masks still covering their skeletal jaws.

"Look at this, Star, more petrolheads." Brooke pointed to the rear of a Mini where the fuel cap was missing. On closer inspection we found that a large number of cars were minus the fuel caps, along with the contents of their tanks. It's become a regular sight by now. Whoever has taken it, needs a hell of a lot.

The wind was starting to pick up and the sharp gusts carried lumps of sleety rain. Grey clouds had appeared over Raincliffe Woods and rolled closer like an alien spacecraft, so we decided to find shelter and eat some lunch (such as it was).

Graham School was conveniently close and much to Brooke's annoyance had not sustained very much damage. ("Half of Scarborough's fallen down, and yet this fucking place is hardly scratched.") We snuck inside just as the clouds burst and soaked the weedy playgrounds and surrounding fields. The corridors echoed back our footfalls as we crept through, checking out the classrooms, cupboards, lockers and (shock, horror) actually finding a few useful items to tick off. Everything I looked at seemed to regurgitate an old memory, and it didn't help that the place still smells the same as it always did: glue, fishy textbooks and methane (particularly around the science block where they once trusted us with Bunsen burners). My mind can't accept seeing B-Staircase without fifty kids cramming their way up and down like it's a Mexican Bull Run.

"Ah, to be a teenager again," whispered Brooke.

"You miss it?"

"What, being horny, angry, depressed, and spotty? Nah, I did my time. That was enough."

It's difficult to believe I was only here for five years…it felt like an entire lifetime. Brooke has significantly less nostalgia, she only attended lessons "when I felt like it," and was apparently expelled at age fifteen for selling weed during lunchtimes ("Mr Carlton-Perry was definitely my best customer").

We've taken cover in a classroom to eat our tins of cold mushroom soup and a couple of soggy KitKats (which we found at the bottom of a vending machine). I did Year 11 history in here. Far and away my best subject. My happy place. Brooke's happy too at the moment, I think. She's playing Keepy Uppie with a globe of the world, trying to break her record of thirty-six.

It's dark outside and the hail is scraping the windows, but hopefully it'll move over soon. Our next destination is decided. A back-up plan of sorts. We're heading down to Falsgrave, to the pharmacy and shops around there. If they've been cleared out, as we suspect they will have, then we'll cut our losses and leave town this afternoon. Be well away by dusk. Maybe head south for Filey or Bridlington, stopping at the caravan parks in between.

Anywhere but here.

10

The fundamentals of survival are actually quite straightforward. You can go three weeks without food, three days without water and three minutes without air. Therefore, the top priorities are, to have a clean water source and plenty of nutritious food, and of course to keep breathing, which I decided, as I was sat in that empty auditorium reeling from Brooke's breaking news, to keep on doing. After all, it wasn't the end of the world. It wasn't judgement day or Armageddon or the apocalypse. Four horsemen weren't about to ride in from the A64. Planet earth would keep on spinning, with or without the human race, and I decided to keep spinning right along with it. For as long as time and fate (if there is such a thing) would allow.

So yes, quite simple. Air, water, food...and there's warmth, that's also a priority, and so is shelter. Fortunately, I wasn't trapped on a frozen lake in Antarctica or in the middle of the Arabian Desert. There are plenty of sheltered spaces around, and as long as I did all the necessary checks to ensure they were empty and/or structurally sound, they were easy pickings. As was the availability of matches and firelighters and all that useful stuff (though the ability to build a fire from scratch is something I pride myself on). Same goes for canned and bottled goods. Same goes for replacement clothes and blankets. Same for tools and equipment.

Yeah, yeah, I'm stating the obvious. If you're somehow reading this, you've survived thus far and it's your day-to-day existence. But I'm making it a thing because for a period of weeks (months?) after first encountering Brooke Barden, survival was my primary focus. I gathered up all the books I could carry and kept them categorised in the lockers in my room at the SJT. Wiseman's SAS Survival Guide, several St John Ambulance's First Aid manuals and Eckhart Tolle's The Power of Now, to name but a few. I studied them, harder than I had ever studied for my GCSE's or A Levels, and unlike much of my formal education, I was able to put what I had learned to practical use. I came to think of it as Nova's ART of survival. A = Adaption – accepting the current situation and adapting my thoughts and actions to deal with it. R = Readiness - planning ahead for any changes in circumstances so I might be prepared. T = Tools - you've got to have the right gear to hand, otherwise, well, you're trapped in a snowstorm, walking in blind circles until you drop face first into the ice and slowly freeze to death.

And just like that, all my stupid worries were gone. As a kid I'd had so many, all of the time: was I getting too fat or thin, would I ever get into university, would I ever earn enough to buy a house or a car, would mum find out about me and Matthew and hit the roof, was my period late, was my period early, would mum expect me to get married and have kids (I'd done plenty of babysitting for the Lomax siblings on Cornelian Drive, and had no desire to go down that road), was Jenny avoiding me, did I write too many lists, was I OCD, was I ADHD, would I ever make it as a teacher?...BOOM. Gone. Vanished. There's really no time for worry when you could literally die of hunger or thirst, or exposure, or from an infected cut. Day to day endurance took all my time and energy, and I had never slept better as a result.

So, I was OK. No longer waiting for help that wouldn't come. I was alive and I was organised, and I was learning. And, dare I say it, I had also managed to save another life and felt quite good about that (if not so much the person). And I had all this fairly well in hand. Aaaand, I'm waffling now! I never wrote what I'm about to write in my other diaries. It was too far away then. It was among the vault full of memories I'd been happy to keep locked up. But now I'm back in Scarborough, and those memories are crawling free. To face them is like peeling off a scab and sticking the wound in a bucket of salt. Does that make sense? Probably not.

The railway station was just across the road from the theatre, but I hadn't gotten around to investigating it yet. I figured there might be some tools stored there that could come in handy, and even if there wasn't, it had been a couple of years since I'd caught a train from there and I fancied another look, given its significance as a piece of Scarborough's past. It opened in 1845 (although the most recognisable section – the frontage and clocktower with its domed roof – weren't added until 1882). By all accounts, when the first train came in – all thirty-five coaches of it – fifteen thousand people were watching. That many bodies, all crowed together...to think about it now gives me anxiety.

I was getting used to the quiet, but it was still eerie to stand on the empty platform, no commuters, no ticket inspectors, no muffled announcements, no train horns, no pigeons chirping away among the steel trusses overhead. There was just a single empty train parked on platform three…no, not quite empty, halfway down the carriage was a corpse slumped over one of the tables, long dark hair masking its face – I was getting used to that too.

There wasn't much in the way of supplies. The Pumpkin Cafe and vending machines had long been emptied, and due to burst pipes and water damage, most of the tools I found were rusted and blunt. The doors on the first carriage had been forced open, so I hopped aboard for a quick once over. There was no smell of decay as I'd expected, just the distant hint of diesel. I walked slowly down the carriage checking the seats and baggage racks. Not a crumb. It had been thoroughly cleaned, probably during the third lockdown. I noticed there were no *reserved* tickets in the slots on top of the headrests. Why would there be? This train was well and truly terminated. I held my breath as I passed the occupied table and continued towards the toilet wondering if I might find a container or two of soap.

"Hello?"

I think I yelped. I certainly jumped and spun around. The body wasn't a body at all. He was sitting up now, leaning comfortably back in his chair, his elbows resting on the table, his dark brown eyes fixed on me.

"Sorry," I muttered. Again, my voice scratched due to its lack of use. "Didn't think you were—"

"Warm." He grinned. A wide grin. Somehow too wide.

I didn't know what to say to that. He'd been so still and silent. In the end I said, "Are you OK? Not hurt or anything? I'm a first aider."

"I'm not bad," he said. "Just hungry, that's all."

"Yeah, there isn't a lot here is there? They must've emptied the place out."

"We did. A while ago."

"We?"

He nodded. He was probably late twenties, early thirties. Bigger than me, but not by much. "Before we were furloughed."

"Oh, you worked here?"

"Pushed the trolley mostly."

"Really? Must've been—"

"Boring," he said. The grin frozen on his lips. "Not like now. What about you?"

"I worked at…" I stopped myself before I could say the theatre. "…University. Hull. Student. Was, until this."

He glanced out of the window at nothing. "Everything's spoiled now."

"It's been hard," I agreed. "But we've got to keep going."

He appeared not to have heard. "It's going rotten, it's putrid and it stinks."

"Well, yeah. Some of it, but a lot of the tinned stuff still has years on it. Same with the dried food." I pointed in the general direction of Tesco. "And there's still a fair bit of it around, if you know where to look."

"It's not the same thought."

"No, but, erm?"

"Ben."

"Ben. You have to accept that. Accept and adapt, it's the art of survival."

He cocked his head. "That what?"

"Oh, just some silly thing I came up with. Nova's Art of survival. A is for adaption. The R is for readiness. You know, being prepared for—"

"Nova?"

I could've kicked myself. My name out of his mouth felt kind of wrong, though I didn't know why. "Yes, it means star."

"I know." He glanced out the window again. "You alone Nova?"

"Course not." I said at once. "My boyfriend's nearby. And my three brothers. Older brothers. They're checking out the ticket office, I think. Should be in here soon."

"You have family? They made it?"

"They did. We were...lucky."

He nodded. "Family is everything. I don't know what I would've done if mine had died."

"Oh, well, I'm glad they're OK. It's really good knowing there's survivors out there. Especially families."

"Especially families. Especially mine. And it's growing every day you know."

"Um. Right....and speaking of which, they'll be wondering where I am. My brothers I mean. I'd, I'd better go."

"Maybe I'll see you around, Nova."

"Maybe. Goodbye."

I should've backed up to the door - I know that now - but instead I turned my back to him and that was when he took his chance.

I was shoved hard between the shoulder blades and went straight into the plastic edge of a seat back. Immediately felt warmth running over my mouth and chin. I heard his voice hot against my ear.

"You're not rotting, Nova. You're fresh."

I screamed but it sounded so quiet and distant, and I knew there was no one else within hearing distance.

"Shhhhhh." There was a sickening tug on my ponytail and my head was forced back, then slammed into the chair again. I saw fireworks against a starless sky, and I was on my stomach, the blood from my throbbing nose staining the blue carpet. My arms were jammed beneath my chest, my watch, long dead, was digging into my sternum.

Another hit. The solid rubber of a polished boot. The breath was forced from my body. Again and again, he bought his foot down on my back and ribs, only stopping when I ceased trying to crawl away. His strong arm gripped my shoulder and dragged me over. The grey carriage roof swam near, and then blurred, and then it was out of sight as he loomed closer. My arms were free now and I flailed them wildly, trying to push him away, but he caught my wrists and held them in an iron grip, then dropped to his knees straddling me and pinned them onto the cold ground. I could feel his erection digging at my stomach, and that face, that wide grinning mouth almost touching mine. His tongue snaked out and he dragged it over my nostrils, then over my cheeks and down my chin, his warm drool coating my flesh. When he backed up, I could see his lips, clown-like with the red of my blood. He licked it all off and his thyroid pulsed as he swallowed it down. "Mm. And I thought today would be boring."

My arms were suddenly free again, though they felt like cold stone tied to elastic bands. His nails were at my neck, on my blouse, grasping at the material around the collar, pulling, tearing. The broken buttons fell around me. I swung my arms once more, managing to rake three lines across his cheek, but he barely flinched. He raised the palm of his right hand and slapped me hard. My head rocked to the left. My bruised, tender nose throbbed, and fireworks exploded once again.

His dark eyes dropped slowly down. Not to my breasts as I would've expected, but to the exposed skin above. "Fresh," he gasped again. "Fresh and dark. Not tried that yet."

He ducked forward, out of my view and I just remember the agony as his teeth sank deep between my neck and shoulder. His head jerked, his jaw clicked, and when he straightened, a lump of my skin was dripping between his teeth. He sucked it into his mouth and chewed slowly and thoughtfully like it was a rare steak. As he swallowed, I heard the faraway clatter of glass, and wondered if it was something breaking inside me. My mind? Perhaps that would be for the best. Perhaps a mercy.

He bared his stained teeth and nodded appreciatively, and then he lowered his face once more for another taste. Once again, the carriage roof filled my vision before turning dark, and a fleeting shadow passed before my eyes. There was a horrible wet, crunch, and I squeezed my eyes shut and waited for a fresh bout of pain...which never hit. Of course, he'd ripped through the nerves, he was down to the bone, chewing through to the marrow. Another crunch. Then a bubbly gurgle. His thighs were tight against me, and they were now juddering violently. In fact, his whole body was shaking, and I could feel the sweaty heat radiating from him.

I opened my eyes.

He hadn't taken a second bite at all. He had straightened. He was staring out in surprise. Not quite at me, but through me. He was no longer grinning. Another flash of shadow and something smooth and red crashed into the side of his head, sinking beneath the mop of hair and possibly the skull beneath. He gasped and swayed side to side. Crimson saliva bubbled from his mouth. A face appeared next his. It took me a moment, but I remembered the Golden Retriever gnawing at the skinny leg. Her lips hovered by his ear, the same way his had done so at mine.

"End of the line, you sick fuck." Brooke Barden held up the weapon: the emergency hammer that she'd wrenched free from its holder next to the window. With a war cry, she swung with all her strength and found the target. His right eyeball popped from the socket and swung to and fro like a bauble on a Christmas tree. He toppled sideways and landed in the footwell between two seats, laying crumpled among his pooling blood.

Brooke threw the hammer on the nearest table and with a grimace, wiped her hand down her top, removing the stains and clumps of hair. "Alright, I'm Brooke." She reached out towards me. "I know bugger all about first aid, but, other than this dipshit, I'm the only one here, so I'll have to do. Have I got your consent?"

11

I took her hand, and we made it off the train and onto the platform. Every step caused my muscles to scream for mercy. It wasn't much better for Brooke who was still limping from the dog attack. Once clear of the carriage, the world grew unbearably heavy and I collapsed like a Jenga tower, then woke facedown on the damp platform.

"Shit, what do I do, Star, what do I do?"

Brooke rolled me onto my back and attempted (I think) to twist me into the recovery position. As she did so, a low guttural cry rang out through the station and for a moment my pain was gone, replaced with raw terror as I lurched up and stared towards the train.

"Oh my god," Brooke recoiled. "That's gross."

Ben was there in the doorway, crawling on his belly like a worm cut in two. There was a dark trail behind him, most likely from his bladder and bowels. The right side of his face was painted red, but even worse, a flap of his scalp was hanging down, and I'm sure I saw fragments of bone stuck in his hair. He slithered through the door, one eye on me, the other swinging madly. He grasped at the first step, lunged for the second, then slipped forward and with a final growl, vanished down the gap between the train and the platform.

Brooke hobbled over and knelt by the steps, watching for nearly a minute. She stood back up and turned to me. "Not good, dude. I think I'd better call him an ambulance...oh no, wait, there aren't none. Oh well." Then she crossed to the nearest bin and vomited into it.

She gave up on the recovery position and asked if I wouldn't mind laying across the nearest bench so she could "take a proper look, and that." Even in my woozy, weakened state, I wanted out of there, no matter how much it hurt.

"Family." I manage to say. "Ben's...Maybe...Look for him."

Brooke glanced around. "Alright. But I need you to walk more than five steps without wimping out on me. Can you do that?"

We made it across Westborough, my arm draped over Brooke's shoulder as she supported my weight. Things went dark for a while and when I came to, we were inside the theatre foyer.

"Where's your stuff," she asked. I muttered directions and when I awoke again, I was in the staffroom laying across my makeshift bed. I was down to my underwear (which was a relief – I'd been able to smell his cologne on my clothes) and Brooke was frantically rifling through my supplies, throwing anything that appeared useful at my feet. I directed her to the relevant kit and recommended which books might help her out, during which she managed a smile. "You're a massive nerd, aren't you Star."

I don't remember much after that. I know she gave me some pills - painkillers and antibiotics - and I fell in and out of consciousness. When I resurfaced sometime later, a lot of the pain was gone. My entire shoulder had been bandaged and my bruised ribs were covered in Koolpaks. Brooke was resting against the wall, her hair stuck down with sweat and dark circles around her eyes. When she saw I was awake she rushed over. "OK?"

I nodded.

"Thank fuck. I thought I'd screwed up."

"No, you helped. How you know where I was…how you know I was here?"

"I'm just a genius," she said. "Aaaaand when we last met you were wearing a top with the SJT logo on it. So that was a bit of a giveaway."

Of course. I'd been wearing my old uniform that day (as my other clothes were hung up in the McCarthy drying).

"Plus, I've been stalking you a bit." She bit her lip. "Soz, that's probably not the best word to use, given what just happened. But yeah, I did *that* a bit. I hoped we'd chat again at some point, but I wasn't sure you'd just kick my arse instead, so I kept my distance."

"Wouldn't have."

"Yeah, I know that now."

"But, but why, follow?"

"I dunno. You seemed to have it together. The places you went, places you got stuff. Seemed to make sense, so I kind of just copied you. It paid off. You've really got it together."

"I'm stupid. Really, really stupid."

She was taken aback. "No, you're not."

"I should've been more careful. I thought I had it all figured out."

"Oh, what *him*? Totally not your fault."

"Shouldn't have turned my back. Shouldn't have even talked to him. Shouldn't have even got on that train without properly knowing—"

"He was a fucking creep. It's not your fault, you hear me. Not. Your. Fault?"

I wasn't convinced but I was too drowsy to talk anymore, so I just nodded. She grabbed a box of Tramadol and gave me one.

"Sleep as long as you want. I'll stay up, as long as necessary. I'll be here when you wake up."

That made me feel even more awful. "Look, when I left you, you know, in newsagents, I didn't mean—"

"Stop!" She held up her hands. "Here's the deal, since we're pretty much even on all other counts. I'll forgive you for sodding off that night, if you forgive whatever embarrassing shit that I said or did when I was drunk."

"You don't remember?"

"Dude, all I remember is the three day hangover and vowing to never touch that shit again. And guess what? I haven't. So do we have a deal?"

We didn't exactly shake on it, but managed to brush fingers, then I lay back to sleep.

Yes, Brooke was there when I woke up. She had popped out briefly, she said, to get food and new clothes for me, but she was there. And she was there the day after, and the day after that. We talked. A lot. She wanted to know all about me, and I opened up completely, telling her things that until now, I wouldn't have even written in a diary. I told her about my life before the pandemic, my mum, Matthew, Jenny and my other friends, school, work, the nightmares I'd been having, my fears about leaving the theatre. For someone as loud as her I was surprised at how well she listened. Had things not gone the way they had she would've made an awesome therapist.

It was probably a week later when I forced myself up off that bed and put on the fresh clothes, and we sat together by the front window, chewing toffee popcorn and watching the darkened streets. I avoided looking towards the station. To even think about that place bought on panic attacks. Brooke knew this, so kept me distracted. On this particular evening, she returned the favour and filled me in on her own history.

12

"Mark was in Year 11, I was a Year 7. I didn't much care cos I was in love. He was already hooked on a lot of stuff, and pretty soon I was hooked too. But so what? I was in love. I desperately had to get away from my folks, so when he got a flat on Belgrave Terrace, I moved in with him as soon as I could. We were near the far end, close to the railway line so there would be a mini earthquake every time the Scarborough to York rumbled past. I didn't care, I was in love. So, I got expelled - St Augustine's, Scalby, and finally Graham – but I already had a job running drugs around town. Mark was the one with the contacts and the money, not that I'm sticking it all on him Star, my fuckups are my own, but I did what he told me. Why wouldn't I? I was in love. I worked a lot of normal jobs too, you know, to supplement our income and that. Cooplands, Boyes, Winking Willy's, The Grand, The Royal, The Opera House Casino, Casino Royale (not the movie, I mean the slotties on the seafront). Anyway, you name it, I got fired from it. Meanwhile, me and Mark got married at the registry office, a few of his mates were there as witnesses. After that, we had a massive piss-up at Spoons. I was only sixteen, but I had no second thoughts, after all, I was...well you know by now. And so what if I got the odd blackeye or fat lip...or the grazed knuckles from where I'd fought back. So what if we lived in chip fat smelling squalor. So what if I was at constant risk of getting busted - if not by the cops, then by one of Mark's competitors – but I just didn't care. You can put up with a lot when your only thoughts are on the next fix. And when you're in love.

Eventually, my luck ran out. I got caught with more than just weed, and since I was no longer a minor, and since I already had a shit load of convictions, and since I'd refused the cavity search, aaaand I'd refused to give the police any names or handles or addresses, I got put in juvie. A four-year stretch. Maybe three if I behaved myself. But I was willing to take the fall, remember, I was in love.

Only, turns out, I really wasn't. Lust? sure, I was horny as hell back then. Loneliness? Absolutely. But love? Nah. It took some, like, real, proper sobriety to realise that. It took weeks of detox and dry heaving into a bucket. It took spending twenty-three hours looking at the same four walls, with all those thoughts and memories whizzing past like shooting stars.

So then the pandemic spreads, right, and everyone's coughing and sneezing and wheezing. A lot of poor sods get taken away in bags, and then many of the staff stop showing up for work, and the place is dead quiet and soon I gather that my sentence is up. I leave New Hall behind, and I come back here. It took weeks or I reckon it felt that way. At first, I 'borrowed' a car and tried to drive it over here, but there were so many roadblocks (no one manning them at this point, obviously), I ended up getting out and walking. Tell you what, having to find safe places to squelter in at night was really...What? Squelter? Oh, it's a cross between squat and shelter. Course it's a word! Surely? Oh. Oh well. Anyway, I squ...I did that thing at night and walked during the day. Got blisters and everything. I saw a lot of shit out there. Just outside York there was loads of, like, military vehicles parked up. Nearby a massive pile of bodies – seventy or eighty at least – all swollen and torn apart by bullets. Probably some sort of riot or protest. Oh. My. God. The smell. And so many maggots and flies. I didn't stick around. There was similar stuff near Malton. In one field it looked like a mass suicide; They had all drunk poison or something. Further on, Scampston or somewhere, a plane, a big one like a jumbo jet, had come down right over the road and gone up in flames.

I get back to Scarborough, right, and it's a ghost town. So, so quiet, like it was for you. I get to the flat and there's no passing trains. There's none of Mark's RnB blaring out, no rugby on the telly, and there's none of his shitty mates slapping me on the arse every time I walked by. Mark *was* there but he was long gone. I finally realised why he'd never bothered to visit me, and hardly ever wrote. Clearly, he'd been getting high on his own supply, and during one of the lockdowns, he'd gone *too* high. Right into the stratosphere where there's no sodding oxygen. He was sat against the wall by the fireplace. His jeans were rolled up and he only had one sock on. Stuck in the green skin between his big and second toe was a syringe. Still full by the looks of it. Maybe the effort of stretching for it had been the final straw for his heart...maybe...or maybe not. I see movement in his chest. Yeah, his Walking Dead T-shirt is rippling. No way he could look and smell like that, and still be alive. Stupidly, I lean down to check his pulse, and a rat the size of my head scurries out, dragging a string of intestines with it. I rushed out into the streets, gagging like I had an eight incher down my throat and once there, I decided to never go back. If I'd still had my wedding ring, I would've taken it off and thrown it away dramatically like they did on telly.

And you know what? You know what I felt? Relief. I know that's fucked up, given what happened. All the people who didn't deserve it. But I'm just being honest, right. I felt relief for the first time in well...forever. And I hit the town and partied like I was eighteen again. And like a dumb, stupid bitch, I almost end up as dead as my late husband. But then, I didn't. Thanks to you. So yeah, that, that's...ARE YOU SLEEPING?"

I assured Brooke that I wasn't. I'd had my eyes closed but listened in pity, amusement and horror. The latest round of medication was kicking in and I was ready to go and sleep it off. She came with me, not having to hold me up anymore, but making sure I didn't fall. As we walked, I noticed she was no longer limping.

"I think I'm done with this," she said suddenly.

"Oh." I did my best to hide my surprise (and dare I say it, my disappointment). "I appreciate you telling me. By all means, take what you want when you do go—"

She laughed. "No, what I mean is, I'm done with this town. I want out."

Again, a stab of melancholy. I knew Brooke and I would have to go our separate ways at some point, but I was getting used to having her around, not just because I was still so scared, and not because she'd been so helpful, but because for the first time in my life, I had someone I could talk to. I mean properly talk to.

"You not convinced? Think of what's out there, Star. Could be fun, know what I mean?"

"Could be horrific. All those awful things you saw, and that was just a narrow stretch of Yorkshire. Think about what else must have happened, in the cities, in the towns. Could be so—"

"Horrific? Yeah, but that's life." She pushed the staffroom door open and stepped aside so I could enter. "Certainly *my* life so far. I just keep thinking, if I'd caught it...if I'd died there in that cell, what would my life of added up to? A shitty marriage, no real mates and a criminal record as long as a tapeworm. I reckon I don't deserve this second chance, but I got it all the same, and I don't want to waste it this time. Besides, it wasn't *all* like that – out there I mean - and it's a big bloody country. I reckon I wanna see a bit more of it, to actually *live* you know what I mean? Before we're extinct altogether."

Maybe it was the effects of the Tramadol, but I was suddenly intrigued. A change of scene. New places. New horizons. And not having to be reminded of all those painful events that I was trying so hard to forget. Surely that would be easier when I wasn't within spitting distance of the places they happened.

"Then you should," I said, climbing under the blankets. "If that's what you want, and yes, maybe I'll do the same one day."

Brooke laughed harder. "Why do you reckon I'm telling you in the first place?"

"What?"

"Say I skip town, right? You fancy tagging on for a bit? You'd be more than welcome."

"You want me around?"

"Well duh. I wouldn't say so if I didn't. It wouldn't have to be forever. If we were to get sick of each other and that, we can go off on our separate ways."

"Well, yes..."

"Anyhow, it's early days, and you need to sleep. But you give it some thought, alright? You give it some thought and let me know."

By my bed, I had an upturned cardboard box as a makeshift table. Laying on top was my old phone: always within reach, even though the battery was empty and it would never ring again. It *did* continue to vibrate, or at least I kept thinking it did. Kept feeling it like an amputated limb (or a missing chunk of skin). I stared at it now and I considered Brooke's offer. And I realised I didn't need to give it any thought.

13

Time: Late evening.
Location: Flat on Westborough. Top Floor.
Weather: Blustery. Cold.

We're alive. Just.

We reached Falsgrave via Stepney Drive then turned right along Scalby Road. We made straight for the Lawrence House Medical Centre, but even from a distance, we could see that the pickings were slim. Same old, same old, it was all broken windows, graffiti up the walls and crumpled boxes and torn, empty packets scattered among the dead leaves. Cohens Chemist was no better. Same goes for the shops and storerooms along Falsgrave. I have to admit, I wasn't angry or disappointed anymore. It just meant that we could leave. It meant we could leave very, very soon. The only problem was our lack of food. We didn't need much, even just a handful of tins would keep us going for a day or so. That was more than enough time to put some miles between us and Scarborough.

Sainsbury's was just across the road. We went the long way around and snuck down the side, gaining access via a fire door beside the main generator. We had barely passed the tea and coffee isle, when Brooke suddenly grabbed my arm and thrust a finger to her lips. We froze. We listened. She was right, we weren't alone. From behind the rows of empty shelves came a clang, then a low rumble. Something small and metal had been displaced and was now rolling slowly along the tiles. This was soon followed by the gentle padding of small feet. A lot of small feet. Drawing ever closer. I sniffed the air and caught the unmistakable reek of hot, wet fur and raw, meaty breath.

There was no point trying to hide. They'd caught our scent waaay before we'd smelled them. Probably before we'd even crept onto the shopfloor. We didn't hesitate. We ran for the nearest exit, bolting between the checkouts, ducking through the broken windows at the front, and then out into the empty carpark and back up the hill, towards the main road. Snarls and barks cut through the air behind us. I glanced back and wished I hadn't. It wasn't just one or two dogs, it was an entire pack. Fifteen, maybe twenty. All of them big – Great Danes, Alsatians, Retrievers, Rottweilers – all of them experienced hunters. They bounded over the tarmac towards us, rapidly closing the distance. I could see the wild, crazed glare in their eyes, and the strings of spit swinging from their jaws and jagged teeth. I was reminded...no forget it...

Off to the left, the front door to a solicitor's office was swinging open. I yelled to Brooke and we rushed up the steps and fell inside. She grabbed the door and made to slam it.

"Leave it," I yelled.

"Wot?"

I took her arm and pulled her down the hall and through the reception, past a set of stairs and then into a back office. Growls filled the rooms behind, along with the desperate scrabbling of unclipped claws on smooth parquet, as the furry, sweaty bodies lurched through, each one trying to get to us before its companions. I slammed the office door, looked for an interior lock and found nothing.

"The desk," I yelled. "Barricade."

Brooke pointed towards the window - glass broken, easy escape - but with my insistence she grabbed hold of the heavy, mahogany desk and scraped it across the floor and against the door. At the same moment, a solid weight slammed against the other side, followed by another and another. Then came the frantic scratching of claws and teeth on wood. I turned to Brooke who, of course, had begun to laugh.

"Get as much stuff against this door as possible. They cannot get though."

"You think!" she shrieked.

I crossed to the window and used the leather spine of a heavy law book to knock out the remaining shards, before climbing out into the yard. I glanced back. Brooke was throwing everything she could against the door, laughing hysterically as she did so.

I bolted down the alleyway, knocking aside several stinking wheelie bins in my haste, before jumping the wall and returning to the main road. I charged up to the front door once again, praying that all the attackers were still inside trying to claw their way through to Brooke. I was in luck for now, but their hacking barks were almost deafening as I reached the top of the steps. I gripped the cold doorknob and pulled it shut. It didn't click, and with a horrible high creak it begun to swing inwards again. I noticed the broken locks and the footprints against the outer wood. At some point, someone had kicked it open. (Course they had!) I reached inside and pulled the door shut again, just as the

Great Dane bounded out from the reception and bared down on me. Its eyes were red, its nose slick with snot and blood. It rammed the door and I was almost thrown backwards down the steps, only stopping myself by grabbing hold of the black railing beside the path. The door was starting to swing open again, and I lunged for it and held on tight.

An idea. I threw off my rucksack and with my free hand I rifled inside and grabbed the length of rope. I tied one end around the doorknob, pulled it taut and wrapped the other around the railings, winding it, again and again. Thank heavens, the door held, despite the furious animal butting it from within.

With my heart in my mouth and my lungs at my feet, I retraced my steps around the back and found that Brooke had pretty much stripped the room bare and shoved it up against the door. She screamed when I called out her name, then cackled again as she rushed over and climbed over the sill to join me.

"They're trapped," I said. "Hopefully."

She gave me a tight hug. She was sweating as much as me. "Clever. I thought we were Chum."

"I just knew if we locked them outside, they'd wait for us to come back out. They might wait for days."

"Hairy bastards."

"Luckily, they must've fed in the supermarket before we got there."

"You reckon?"

"Yeah. If they were properly hungry, we never could've outrun them. They were just playing with us."

"Man's best friend? What a load of toss."

We set off, back towards Westborough, keeping our eyes and ears peeled for anymore strays.

"Poor things," I said.

"You wot!"

"They're just trying to survive like us."

"Nah, they're evil. Mad. Probably got locked inside with their dead owners, ended up having to chow down on them. Ever since, they've had a hunger for human flesh."

We passed by the main door. The noise from within had abated. Brooke jogged up the steps and examined the rope, running a finger along it. "Nice one. Should hold. With any luck they'll turn on each other now."

I hated the idea of them starving to death in there, but what else was I supposed to do?

By the time our adrenaline had well and truly worn off, we were both exhausted and more than a little on edge. Not only that, but another sundown was turning the sky a greeny red. Falsgrave was a loss, and there was no way were we venturing back inside Sainsbury's (or any other supermarket for that matter). There was nothing for it but to squelter in town for yet another night.

So we've got a flat not far from Westborough Methodist Church. Normally we'd avoid setting up camp on the top floor of a building, as it makes the escape route more challenging, but from our current position, we have a decent lookout up and down the road. Plus, we've shoved a heavy wardrobe against the front door, should Cujo and friends somehow make it up here. There were two skeletons in the main bedroom so we're keeping to the lounge. One happy find was a small camping stove under the kitchen sink, and we were able to share a tin of hot oxtail soup and some butterbeans. Not enough, but it'll have to do.

All the clothes here are way too big for us, and we're too cold and tired to start heating water and doing the laundry, so we're having to keep our torn, sweaty ones on for the time being. There's plenty of lynx deodorant in the bathroom so we've doused ourselves in that. It's made us smell like a teenage boy's changing room, but it's something at least.

Neither of us could sleep, so using the flickering light from a candle, we read aloud some articles from a stack of The Scarborough News which Brooke had found on the top of a bookcase. Some highlights include: the unveiling of the Open Air Theatre by Queen Elizabeth II in 2010, the demolishing of the Futurist Theatre: 2018, a Civil War enactment at Scarborough Castle in 2016 and the Centenary of the WWI Bombardment in 2014. A lot of this I can remember quite clearly, but it still, somehow, feels like ancient history. We did manage a few laughs at some of the smaller stories: two neighbours rowing over an overgrown hedge on Beechville Avenue. Harry Merchant, of no fixed abode, trying to sue the local authorities because a seagull had snatched his pork pie. And yes, a particular Brooke Barden, of Belgrave Terrace, caught trying to smuggle a miniature bottle of Tequila out of Poundland in her bra.

"Oh my god," she cringed. "What a dickhead."

I gave her the paper and allowed her to tear it into small strips. She did so, then jammed them into her mouth, chewed them into a paste and spat it all out of the window.

"Just when you reckon the past is dead," she said, wiping her black strained tongue on her sleeve, "it comes right back and bites you in the big, fat present."

14

Time: Early hours.
Location: Flat on Westborough.

Noise.

Coming from the town centre, I think. People. Quite a few from the sounds of it. Whistles, cheers, yells (men and women), the smashing of glass. Even heard the distant blast of a car horn at one point. Out the window we can see the occasional torch beam cutting up through the darkness. Just earlier, I thought I heard music too. Just a hint of it on the breeze. Dancing Queen by ABBA.

It started during my watch, but I didn't need to wake Brooke to warn her. The shattering of the usual nocturnal silence had done that. At first, she thought the dogs had escaped until she joined me at the window and listened to the distant voices.

"Shit, it must be Saturday night," she said in a whisper. "All we need now are the police sirens to complete the effect."

I didn't laugh, I didn't smile. I'm scared. Who are they? Locals, or is it a gang passing through? Wreckers like the ones that've caused so much carnage around here. Vandals and murderers.

I can't sleep. Neither of us can. Westborough's still deserted, I'm relieved to say. They probably don't know that we're up here, but I'm not taking any chances. It's not safe to go out, so I heaved more furniture against the front door, while Brooke raided the kitchen for anything and everything with a sharp edge. We're both on watch at the window now, just in case any of them decide to come up.

15

Time: Early morning.
Location: Flat on Westborough.
Weather: Actual sunshine (but it's cold).

It dragged on, but the streets outside remained empty. By the time the dawn sun released its glow, it was over. The only sounds were the squawks from the few remaining seagulls. Everything felt much as it had done so before.

"Maybe they're vampires," said Brooke, and I'm not entirely sure she was joking.

I felt so tired. Drained. I'd lost count of how many nights it had been since I had enjoyed more than a few hours of unbroken rest. The lukewarm Pot Noodle we shared for breakfast did little to raise my spirits. Brooke was acting quiet and awkward. Kept pacing the room and stopping to glance out of the window. To be honest, it was getting on my nerves.

"What is it?"

She turned to me, her blue eyes wide, her lower lip between her teeth. "I wanna check it out."

I just looked at her.

"Something was going on last night. Something's been going on all over this bloody town. I'm just, like...curious."

"Hm."

"I just wanna see what's happening. I know you want out, and I do too, believe me, but I'm just, just—"

"Curious. You already said."

"Come on, Star. A quick look. I won't be long, I swear. I'll be a Ghost."

"No."

She grasped her hands together in mock prayer. "Please. Just an hour."

"I mean, no - you're not going out there alone."

I knew nothing I said was going to change her mind, but it wasn't just that. 'Curious' is definitely the right word, and I was feeling it too. How many are here? Where did they all come from? Where were they staying? What were they doing? So many questions.

We stuffed our bags behind the sofa, then dragged the furniture away from the door and after a careful check around, we left the building via the backdoor. As always, the weedy alleyways provided suitable cover, as did the back streets and yards. We paused regularly to peer over the walls, checking out the main roads nearby. The closer we got to the centre, the more widespread the destruction. It was a depressing sight. I remember how Jenny and I would be out there shopping most Saturday mornings, looking at things we couldn't afford, maybe stopping by Bonnets or The Conservatory or Le Café Jardin for cake. Now all those places were empty, and many more were destroyed. Outside the Yorkshire Building Society, it looked as though someone had had a money fight. Shiny piles of coins covered the ground like frost, along with clumps of wet, faded notes. Thousands of pounds, maybe millions. Such a waste. That kind of cash is great for getting campfires going.

We were passing by the Brunswick when we heard the music again. Not loud, more of an ethereal echo drifting on the morning breeze. We stopped and listened. It had been years since I'd last heard it, but it was unmistakable. Fernando. We followed the sound, heading further into the centre, losing it as we passed between buildings, then hearing it again, a little louder than before. It wasn't until we emerged onto St Nicolas Street, near the burned ruins of the Town Hall, did we realise it was coming from inside The Grand Hotel. But that wasn't all. There were lights too. Proper electric lights. Not many, just a few dotted along the north side, but it answered one of our most pressing questions.

We stayed low and moved slowly through the car park, beneath the long, wide shadow of the hulking structure to our left. We couldn't crawl: the ground was carpeted with glass which crunched beneath our shoes. Every vehicle had been raided, and every petrol tank syphoned. The music was louder now, drifting out of the main entrance. The Winner Takes It All, what else? There were other sounds too. A soft thudding like a small engine. A Generator: That would explain the music, lights and the tang of exhaust in the air.

Brooke grabbed my shoulder and pointed towards the entrance. People. I counted thirteen of them, stood casually on the front steps, some leaning up against the chipped, white pillars. They were talking loudly, laughing boisterously and in between, puffing on fat cigars. Their clothes looked brand new, and many of them were sparkling with silver chains, gold rings, diamond broaches, and designer looking watches. Laying at their polished feet were piles of shopping bags, full to bursting.

You see that? mouthed Brooke. *Vultures.*

The sun was bright now. The music - The Day Before You Came - suddenly cut out and half of the lights snapped off. The group on the steps, having discarded their cigar ends in the gutter, gathered up their bags of loot and disappeared into the building.

"Vultures, I swear to god." Brooke hissed. "Bet they've got Aladdin's sodding cave in there, while we're picking through the shite they've left, and almost becoming dogmeat for our trouble. Come on."

We snuck away, returned to the flat, boiled our meagre water supply and had the last of the instant coffee from Cliff House. I'd never noticed before how sour it tasted. Hardly surprising really; the jar was three years past its use by date. Brooke was pacing again, whispering breathlessly and almost spilling her mug as she did so.

"How many do you suppose are in there?"

"Dozens at least."

"And you reckon it's them that've stripped every goddamn building?"

"Certainly looks that way."

"Cheeky bastards. I bet they've got pills popping out of every orifice." She gulped the last of her drink and dropped the mug into the bin. "You know I used to work there, right?"

"Yes, you've told me."

"Not a great two days if I'm honest, buuuuut, I *do* know my way around."

I knew where this was going, but I didn't stop her.

"And that could be useful, you know, for getting in and out, for getting around without anyone seeing."

Again, I didn't argue. Maybe I was too weary. Maybe I was angry as well. After all, we do what we must to survive, that's a given, but the cigars, the designer trainers, the jackets, the jewellery, the full-to-bursting shopping bags...and the memory of all those ruined, vandalised buildings. All those bare shelves. All that lack of care and respect.

"Best case scenario," Brooke continued, "they're all in bed with hangovers the size of Jupiter. Worst case, there's loads of them up and around, but the place is huge: loads of rooms and stuff to lay low in."

"Worst case scenario," I said. "One of more of those 'vultures', as you call them, are responsible for the Hand's Off man."

"We don't know that." Brooke drew the knife from her belt. "But if that is the case, and they give us any shit," she sliced the blade through the air. "I'll totally Zorro them. I'll cut their nipples off."

And like before, she wanted to go in alone, but I wouldn't let her. We're going in there together. We'll investigate and then decide on a plan of action. Our bags and most of the equipment will be staying here. I found a small Jar Jar Binks rucksack in the closet, which we're using for some essentials: a hammer and screwdriver (in case of any tough locks), a handful of masks, a torch, two candles and matches (in case the torch fails!). And of course, our knives. Brooke wants me to leave the "stoopid" diary here, but I don't want it out of my sight. I'm not losing another one so soon.

16

Time: Mid-morning.
Location: The Grand Hotel. Turret Room.
Weather: Bright, but windy at this height, obviously.

I've never been inside before, but this place is kind of fascinating. It took four years to build and when it opened in 1867, it was the largest hotel in Europe. Easy to believe, it really dominates the south bay. It's in the shape of a massive V, for Queen Victoria. We're currently in one of four dome-shaped towers, that's one for each season of the year. There are twelve floors to represent the months, fifty-two chimneys for the weeks, and three hundred and sixty-five guestrooms for the days. I told all this to Brooke but, of course, she's not impressed. By the time I got around to saying about the six million plus bricks on the outside, and the eleven miles of carpet within, she said she was popping into the bathroom "for some alone time."

Getting in was easy. I *would* say that we broke in, but the fire door – the one just off McBean Steps - was so rotten it practically crumbled apart in my hands. The first thing that hit us was the smell. Damp. So thick and strong, that we donned our masks to avoid breathing in too many spores. We were in the bowels of the hotel. A rat's maze. Corridor upon corridor, some lined with rooms, others leading to kitchens, closets, and lounges. All gloomy. All cold. All dripping. Every wall was smeared with black mould, every carpet sprouted mushrooms. A lot of the pipes had burst down there, causing the ground to squelch underfoot. At one point we had to double back as the descending stairs vanished into a frothy brown lake. Brooke led the way but I'm pretty sure she was as lost as I was. She'd only worked here those couple of days, and there's no way anybody could learn their way about in that time. It was only when the scent of decay had lessened (to be replaced by the hot fumes of exhaust), did she appear to gather her bearings.

We took a concrete stairwell up several levels to find more twisting corridors and numbered rooms and more empty lounges. Somewhere above, we heard the drone of raised voices. Some sort of fight? I hoped they would continue, so the squelching of our shoes would be drowned out. At this level, the smell of petrol burned through our masks, and we soon discovered why: one of the lounge doors was chained up, a newish looking padlock attached. We approached and took it in turns to glance through the narrow window. Rows upon rows of red jerry cans - full by the looks of it - and covering every inch of the floor. Further along we found the remains of an old generator dumped on one of the tables, surrounded by tools. An abandoned repair job? They clearly had enough replacements.

At last, we made it to the lobby. A huge, cavernous space. It must've been so...well *grand* in its day, but now it was spider city. Webs stretched between the pillars and across the ceilings. Everywhere we looked the cream paint was yellowing and peeling off in large flakes, covering the chairs and tables which were worn and rotten. The argument was close by, one of the back rooms behind the reception, two women, mostly incomprehensible. They sounded drunk, or high, or both.

Brooke suddenly gasped and poked my shoulder and pointed towards the Cabaret Ballroom. The doors were ajar, and a narrow slice of light cut inside, illuminating some of the contents. I gasped too.

"No way."

We crept inside, almost collapsing when our eyes had adjusted to the gloom.

"Forget Aladdin," whispered Brooke. "This is fucking Raiders of the Lost Ark."

She was right, but instead of large wooden boxes it was...well everything else. You name it and there's a good chance it was there. *IS* there. The seats had been pulled out and stacked along the back wall and the floor was now crammed with treasure. It was even piled high on the low stage and up against the fire doors to the side. Tins, packets, cans, cartons, tea, coffee, hot chocolate, tools chests crammed full, tents, fishing rods, makeup, toiletries, kitchen utensils, rack after rack of clothes, footwear of every size and description, boxes of vitamins and iron tablets, toasters, microwaves, barbeques, books, boxes and boxes of batteries, DVD's, CD's, Blu-ray's, games consoles, even kids' toys and games. And yes, the contents of doctor's surgeries and pharmacies and hospitals. Everything we could possibly need and so much more.

We must've circled the ballroom twice, weaving in and out of all the shelves, tables, racks and boxes, just staring, our mouths gaping like idiots. Completely distracted. Our guard down. We didn't know we were being watched until it was too late.

"Lovely to see new faces in here."

We jumped. The prescription bottle I'd been examining fell to my feet. She was on the upper gallery looking down at us. We might've fled, but a man and woman had moved into the doorway. Each had a cricket bat in their hands.

"We're just looking," I said. (Pathetic I know.)

"Well go ahead." And she backed away from the rail and vanished from view. Moments later she appeared from behind the stage, straightening the red curtain as she passed. She was probably five feet tall, mousy hair down to her shoulders. Dressed in a baggy cardigan and corduroy trousers.

"You triggered our alarm," she said, and pointed to the walls where motion sensors had been set up.

"We're just looking," I said again.

She laughed. At a guess I would say she was in her mid-fifties. "No need to look so worried, ladies."

"Oh yeah?" Brooke pointed to the doorway. "Then why the fuck are they carrying bats?"

"Same reason you have knives in your belts. Is it just the two of you?"

"No," I said quickly. "We have ten more on their way."

She didn't believe me, that much was obvious. "The more the merrier," she said. "I'm Suzanne, by the way. Those two: Alice and Stevie."

Brooke scoffed. "Your goons?"

"My children, actually."

"I'm…Samara," I said, then pointed to Brooke. "This is Jenny."

"Sure. Sure."

"We heard noises last night and just came here out of curiosity."

"You live here?"

"Used to. Just visiting."

"Well, you're very welcome. *Samara*."

"Thank you," I was managing to keep my voice steady, I think. "But we've got a long way to go before nightfall so—"

"What the fuck is this place?" I could've killed Brooke at that moment.

"It's The Grand Hotel," said Suzanne. "Our home."

"I know *that*. What I mean is," she spun in two massive circles, waving her arms back and forth. "WHAT IS THIS?"

"Just our stores."

"*Just*. There's enough for, like, a million years."

"Not quite. But there is plenty. We need it. There's a lot of us here, *Jenny*."

"You've stripped the town to its bones, and we've wasted three sodding days digging through empty rooms. We almost died out there."

"Is that so? I'm really sorry. It can be dangerous."

"No shit lady. Any of this stuff from Alpamare?"

Suzanne looked confused. "Yes, probably. Why d'you ask?"

"Oh, please."

"No, I'm serious."

"There was a body there," I said, still keeping my voice calm. "Killed."

"No," said Brooke. "Not killed. Murdered. Tortured first. Tortured and robbed."

"And you think *I* did that?"

"Or one of your darling *children*."

The smile left Suzanne's face. "Ugly things have happened, during and after the pandemic. But not because of us."

"Bullshit. You lot take what you want, and if anyone tries to stop you, you mess them up."

"No, you're wrong. We've had casualties too—"

"Then you bring it all back to this shithole, and smoke your cigars, and drink your champagne, play your ABBA, and dance around naked or whatever people like you do."

I gave Brooke, what I hoped was, a gentle nudge. She really wasn't helping. She turned to me. "Wot?"

"Nothing...let's just...calm."

"This isn't some sort of cult, Jenny." Suzanne pointed, once more, to her children. "I prefer to think of this as a family."

"Oh, you mean like the Manson's? Like Myra Hindley and that Brady dipshit?"

In the silence that followed, Suzanne eyed Brooke closely. "You're not Jenny, are you? You're Barden, right? Brooke?"

I felt her tense. "How...you know me?"

"A long time ago. If memory serves, you were caught stealing plushies from Clinton's. I was the store manager at the time. I was the one who apprehended you and phoned for the police."

"Don't remember."

"No? Not surprised. You were on something or other. You were well known back then. Had pride of place in our rogue's gallery."

"Wot?"

"Sorry, the file with all the mugshots. Local criminals, thieves, drug dealers, perverts, that kind of thing. You and your husband. Mark, isn't it?"

"That was a long time ago, Suzanne." I said, before Brooke could lose it again. "A lot's changed since then."

She nodded, keeping her eyes fixed on my friend. "Fair enough." She seemed to relax a little. "I just hoped you would understand a thing or two about desperate times, and our efforts to overcome them." She reached towards me, and I flinched, but instead of touching me she knelt and scooped the pill bottle from between my shoes, and replaced it gently on the table. "When the whole world had seemingly died, and we realised that no one was coming to help us, *those* were desperate times. Those of us that remained had to act or we would've starved. And yes, as you say, we stripped the town. There had to be enough to go around, not just for us, but for anyone else who came to us in need of help. And there were many in those first few months. And to this day, we still welcome a few passers-by. Like yourselves for example."

"But we're not here to—"

"This might be our extinction event, but that doesn't mean we're going to lay down and take it. We must be prepared."

Another silence, longer this time. Suzanne turned to Alice and Stevie and nodded. They lowered their bats.

"And sure, some of the family might've gone overboard at times. Not murder, I can promise you that, but I am ashamed to say there were some binges. Some partying. Not through greed though, but through grief. A coping mechanism. Surely, we've all been guilty of that at one time or another. Tell me I'm wrong?"

We said nothing.

"Exactly." Suzanne rubbed her hands. "So, Brooke and, erm, Samara?"

"Nova."

"Nova. What is it that you need?"

I glanced at Brooke, but she looked too downcast to say anything, so I spoke. "Medical supplies mainly."

"Well, you're in luck. We have some. But I can't just let you walk out of here with whatever you want, it'll give the wrong impression. Like you said, there are bad people out there who will take what they want and leave a trail of destruction behind. Like the poor man in the waterpark. That being said, we are open to trade."

"Us too," I said, and pointed to the small Jar Jar bag on my back. "But we don't have much. And it looks like you already have everything we could offer in return."

Suzanne glanced at her watch (which actually worked). "S'cuse me, I've got some things to get, if you don't mind?" She walked through the stores, and we followed, watching as she grabbed a pack of nappies from one section, then a carton of Oat Milk from another. "There's always work to be done," she said. "Supply runs. Maintenance in the hotel. Cleaning. Finding fuel for the generators, that's a faff. And if you're feeling really brave, there are some vicious strays out there that need putting down." She took a jar of baby food from a tall stack and pocketed it. For a moment I was tempted to offer my babysitting services in trade, but I stayed quiet. "I mean, I could offer you both a position here, long term, but somehow I think you have your hearts set on leaving."

"You're right there," muttered Brooke. "We're done with Scarborough."

"Oh," Suzanne ginned, "this is no longer Scarborough. This is whatever we want it to be."

"You reckon?"

"I *know*. I've lived here all my life. I've seen it fall, and I've seen it rise."

"Shouldn't that be the other way around?" I said.

She just grinned again. "You know, you both look exhausted. Why don't you rest here for a while. We can provide a quiet room, if you like? There are plenty going spare. Grab a few hours of sleep and come to see me later. Maybe, we can work something out."

"No," said Brooke. "I don't trust you. Any of you."

"That's alright Brooke Barden, we don't trust you either. That doesn't mean we can't help each other out." She reached among a waist high basket of tins, grabbing a handful and holding them out to us. More food than we'd eaten in the last week. "By the way, you ladies hungry?"

"We're fine," I lied.

"You sure?"

Silence.

"You said you've wasted three days already, are you really prepared to waste a fourth? Look around you."

And we did. Again.

With the tins in our hands, Alice and Stevie led us up the endless stairs to our designated room (or I think it counts as a suite). The coughing of generators rumbled through some of the floors, accompanied by the smell of smoke. We passed by many occupied rooms. Could hear conversations and music and televisions blaring away. It was all so strange. Like we'd stepped through a portal into the past. Had it not been for the tired decay of the walls around us, I'm sure I would've started to believe it.

Once they left us alone, we slid the bed against the door and tied some sheets together to form a climbing rope. (There's a doable escape route down the outside of the dome, then across the roof and onto the fire escape, but that's a LAST resort.) There are small porthole-like windows on the curved walls, just wide enough to squeeze through. It's a shame they're so caked in dried bird poo, as the sea view would've been amazing.

We've eaten now, hot food too – they leant us a camping stove - and we even manged to sleep for a bit. I won't lie. I feel so much better.

"OK," I said, once Brooke had finally emerged from the bathroom. "Try and see it from their point of view. They've survived, but most of their families, friends, colleagues, etcetera, haven't. They're scattered around town. Grieving. Lost. Alone. The best alternative to being a Ghost or a Nostalgalite, is to move in here. Part of a team. Part of a 'family'."

"And become Wreckers instead," Brooke said. "Don't tell me you actually trust them?"

"No more than you do. But if they mean what they say, you know, about trading...about us doing a few jobs for them and in return we get the rest of our list, then I'm willing to consider it. It worked out last time."

"What the old couple in Cambridgeshire? Not quite the same, dude. We *liked* them, and vice versa."

"And I like the contents of that ballroom, don't you?"

"Well, duh."

"Obviously it depends on the jobs they ask us to do, right? I'm not about to empty five-hundred toilet buckets into the North Sea."

"Maybe Suzanne wants someone to hold her baby while she goes out on the town for a night of pillaging."

"You saw the baby stuff?"

"Yep. Didn't realise people were still breeding these days."

"Me neither. But given their access to supplies, I suppose it makes sense."

"Dunno...it could be a rock with a face scrawled on it in lipstick. Wouldn't be the first time."

"So, you're OK with this? Meeting with Suzanne, negotiating?"

"We'll see." Brooke patted the knife again.

"And if we don't agree with her terms, we go. Out the door. Out the town."

"Gladly."

17

Location: Turret Room.
Time: Dark.

Why didn't we just leave when we had the chance? We were all set to go. Had a route planned out and everything. We could've been miles out of town by now. Could've got what we needed elsewhere (in places that hadn't been decimated). We never would've come here. We never would've seen...bloody hell, why am I so stupid? Brooke has resumed her pacing, only stopping to listen at the door and to check that her knife is to hand, and of course, looking over at me with that worried expression. I can't blame her. I can hardly write properly; my hand is shaking so much. But what else is there to do? Nothing until we can attempt our escape, and that won't be for another few hours.

So earlier, Stevie and Alice banged on our door, waking us. We scrambled to move the bed back from the door before opening it. They asked if we'd had enough time to think over their mother's proposal, and if so, would we please pop along to her room and speak with her. We agreed and went along, through another warren of passageways, these ones considerably cleaner than the rest of the building. There were more people up and about by now. impeccably dressed, healthy and groomed. They stood aside and watched us with interest as we passed them by.

Suzanne looked genuinely happy to see us. She invited us into her room. It was huge. A family suite or something like that. The walls were a shiny cream, with just a hint of fresh paint in the air. The views over the town looked spectacular from the spotless windows. The green curtains either side looked new. The door clicked shut behind us, Stevie and Alice hovered there. I noticed the pack of nappies laying by the bed, and a scattering of baby food jars on the desk by the wall. I looked around for any sign of a baby (or a smooth rock painted with lipstick). There was neither, but by the far window, a figure was sat in the armchair, staring at the window. No, not sat exactly, slumped. Cocooned in blankets, with a baseball cap pulled low. An elderly relative maybe? Suzanne's dad?

"You've rested," said Suzanne with a wide smile. Too wide. It sent a sharp chill up my spine, but I didn't quite understand why. "You look so much better. It's amazing how things can change, don't you think? Before all of this I just worked. I worked and I worked. I wanted to provide for everyone, give them the things I'd never had when I was a girl. Problem was, I worked so much I barely saw my children, and then eventually they left school and got jobs and lives and moved out. My husband went too, back to Liverpool with his new partner. It felt silly to me, rolling around a five-bedroom house all on my own, so I got a flat on Harcourt Place...not so much a flat, more a bedsit – I could walk its length in ten steps. It wasn't really an issue though, I was hardly ever home. I was out working, more diligently than ever. Then the pandemic arrived and I'm suddenly off. And, apparently I'm redundant. I'm in that barely furnished flat, staring at those four magnolia walls for weeks, for months. Alone. Always alone. No way to see my family, not even remotely (I hadn't had time to get the Wi-fi sorted!) I had no interests, no hobbies, no distractions from the painful grind of that passing time. It was then I realised, all that work, all that loyalty, it had been for nothing. I had some savings, sure, but I couldn't even benefit from those since the shelves were empty. The hoarders had moved in like magpies and taken it all for themselves. There was nothing I could do but wait to fall sick. To go to bed and die like everyone else. Only I didn't. Things changed." She cleared her throat. "So, you're happy to stay on and assist us for a few days?"

There was a moment's silence. I think Brooke was waiting for me to speak, but I was distracted, so she spoke for me. "Perhaps."

"That would be lovely."

"But it depends on the jobs."

"Fair enough. I've had a think and I have a couple of proposals, if you'll hear me out?"

"Sure."

Suzanne perched on the edge of the bed, steepling her hands in the lap of her corduroys. "So far, we've focused our gathering on the town centre and the north side. We want to move our attention towards to the south. Starting with The Esplanade. Not the Crown Spa or the other hotels, we've already cleared those. But there are many flats that we've yet to look at. I have a group of volunteers ready and willing, if you care to join them. Let's say a week of work. You go in, you look, you gather up anything that's useful and you bring it back to me." She shrugged. "It's second nature to you ladies, I'm sure."

A bubbly groan rippled from over by the window. Suzanne glanced over. I could see a pale hand, resting over the arm of the chair, narrow fingers curled inwards like claws. I felt that cold stab again, but apparently, I was the only one.

"Sounds simple enough," said Brooke with a shrug. "And in return we get what we need?"

Suzanne nodded. "With our blessing."

"Even tablets and that?"

"If that's your poison Brooke, then yes of course."

Another gurgle. Deep and guttural. Suzanne looked at her watch and then towards Alice. "Feed him, would you, pet."

Alice huffed softly and snatched a jar off the desk and approached the figure. She slid the baseball cap off to reveal a bald, misshapen skull, coated with grey skin that stretched so tightly, it looked ready to tear.

"I do have another proposal," Suzanne continued, her cheeks reddening a little. "Something a little easier. Something, dare I say it, a little more...interesting. If you'll hear me out?"

"Right, go on."

Alice scooped out a pile of the white goo and forced it towards the dark hole of a grinning mouth. He gurgled and recoiled and turned away. The sunlight revealed his face. My stomach twisted, and my head swam. I was sure I was hallucinating, or this was another nightmare and I would soon wake up, screaming. But no, I could feel Brooke tense up as well. I could hear her suck in her breath. This was no dream. There was no waking from it.

"It would be three days instead of the seven." Suzanne smiled again. Her eyes lowered. Leering. I barely noticed. "Three days and nights."

He looked so different now. His right eye had been pushed back in, but it was milky and grey. The side of his head was covered in long scars, not just from the initial injury, but from bad stitching performed by an unsteady hand.

"A few of the family, well, let's just say it's been a while. Quite a long while. Perhaps it's been the same for the two of you. Unless you're both...that way inclined..."

Many of the teeth that had helped form that horrible grin, were now chipped and brown.

"A couple of fresh faces around here – not *just* faces – well, they can always be appreciated. The men, and perhaps some of the girls, might really enjoy what you can do for them."

Alice tried another spoonful, but he recoiled once more and this time he looked straight at us. At me. He stared. Across to the door, over to his mother, onto Brooke, and then back at me. And that one working eye, it seemed to widen. To glare. To pulsate. Surprise? Recognition? Fury?

"And there's nothing I want more than to keep the family happy. Family is everything to me. Everything."

Again silence. It was all coming back. The footprints on my spine. The tearing agony in my shoulder. The indignity of a punishment that was undeserved. *Fresh and dark. Not tried that yet.*

"And they're nice people. There wouldn't be any problems. You'll enjoy every moment, I'm sure."

"NOo."

Every eye turned on Ben. He kept watching me. *And I thought today would be boring.*

"NOOoo..." He opened his mouth. The runny contents sleered down his chin and slopped into his lap in long, phlegmy strings.

"For fucksake," hissed Alice, reaching for a towel and roughly mopping at his mouth.

"Alice!"

"NOOooo..."

I could taste my lunch from earlier. Sweat dripped from under my arms. My mouth was as dry as dust. *Just hungry. That's all. Just hungry.*

"Don't look so surprised you two," said Suzanne, her attention back on us. "We do what we must to survive. A few days of opening up for an appreciative audience, surely, it's a small price to pay."

"VAAa."

My head felt heavy. My ears hurt from all the blood pumping through them. I could barely hear anything above the piercing whistle.

"NOOo..." His hands trembled, more than mine. His clawed fingers reached and grasped at the air around him. "VAAa."

"Alice, how many times." Suzanne turned her head again. "Don't make a meal of that."

"VAAa..."

"Not my fault, mum. He won't keep still."

"Just get on with it, please. So," again to us, "how about it? You think we have a trade?"

"Yeah, you know what? I think we can make a deal." Even in my befuddled state, I was amazed at how calm Brooke kept her voice. Way better than I ever could. I was anything but calm. I was running on thin ice, waiting for the world to fall out from beneath me.

Suzanne leaned forward. Her tongue slipped out and wet her lips. "We can, can we?"

"Yeah, I reckon we're down with that. But tomorrow. After, like, a decent sleep. Right? We're kind of knackered."

"Hm. Sure, lovely. In that case, we should—"

"VAAaaa." There was a clatter. The jar had been knocked from Alice's hand, and its contents now stained the carpet.

"Shit, Ben. What the hell's wrong with you?" Alice looked at Suzanne. "Muuum, tell him."

"NOOo...vvaaa." Ben raised his right hand. His middle finger uncoiled, his joint clicked as the arm straightened. His black nail pointed straight at me. And that left eye, so wide now it was turning bloodshot, it watched.

That was when my internal scream reached fever pitch, and I lost my grip and my legs slipped from under me. I'd like to say it was a clever rouse to get us out of that horrible room, but I'm not that brave and not that smart. I toppled forward and would've hit the floor if Brooke hadn't grasped the back of my top.

Suzanne wasn't leering anymore. She glanced at me, then to her son (who was writhing in his chair like it was on fire), and then back at me again. "She OK?"

"She's just tired. We both are." Brooke pulled me to my feet and yanked my arm over her shoulder. "Just needs rest." She spun us towards the door which Stevie was still guarding. "Now!"

He looked past us, to his mother, who gave a nod.

"Take care of them, would you, pet?"

Back in our room, Brooke lowered me onto the bed where I've been ever since. She pulled the chair from under the desk and forced it beneath the handle.

"Fuck, fuck, fuck, how?" She massaged her temples. "How in the name of hell?"

"Him," was all I could manage.

"I swear, he was on those rails with his brains spilling out. I swear it, Star. I checked. You remember, I made sure. How, just how?"

"We...we have to go."

"Yep, no shit," said Brooke, then she paused and softened her tone. "Soz, I'm just pissed off."

"I'm scared."

"It's alright. We wait for a bit. If it's anything like last night, we can slip out once they're all pissed up. ABBA will keep them all busy. If that doesn't work, we can go over the roof."

"I'm scared. What if he tells them?"

"I doubt it. He's a drooling retard. He's not telling anyone anything."

"He recognised us."

"Nah, I don't think—"

"He recognised me."

"His brain's gone to mush."

"He said my name."

"He didn't, it was just…noise."

"He pointed—"

"No way—"

"We're gonna die."

Brooke managed a smile. "Well, look on the bright side, dude. At least then we won't have to get fingered by a bunch of horny, blinged-up wankers. Did you hear her 'proposal'? Oh. My. God. I'd rather cut out my tongue than stick it in her mousy old bargain bucket."

"But what are we supposed

NO THE DOOR…

That was Suzanne. She knows. She definitely knows.

Managed to shove this under the pillow before we let her in. It's all in here. All about Ben and what he did…what *we* did. If she sees it…so, so stupid.

Anyway, she entered without permission and again, Stevie blocked the doorway. She was trying to look sympathetic, but I could tell it was just an act.

"We were worried, Nova." She approached the bed and placed a damp palm on my ankle. I could smell her sickly-sweet perfume. "I just wanted to check you're alright."

"She's fine," said Brooke. "Just trying to sleep."

"If there's anything you—"

"There isn't." Brooke bit her lip. "But thank you kindly."

"I also wanted to apologise, about before."

"For what?"

"Ben. My son. I understand that his appearance might have…disturbed you. That you might have been a little squeamish."

"No," said Brooke. "We didn't really notice, did we?"

I shook my head. It turned the room upside down.

"That so?" She perched on the bed, her fingers walking slowly over my calf. "It just seemed like you couldn't wait to be out of there."

"No," I croaked. "I just took a turn. Didn't want to be sick on your floor."

"It's alright, pet. He makes me sick too sometimes. Not deliberately."

"She didn't mean it like that," said Brooke. "Some people are born with, stuff. Doesn't bother us. We get it. It's no big deal."

"Oh, but it *is*. For me it is. He wasn't born that way, you see, that was done to him. He was attacked and left for dead. I told you before, Brooke, we've had casualties. My son was one of them. They didn't rob him. They just wanted to kill him. To hurt me, perhaps? We did what we could to treat him. We saved his life, but we couldn't reverse the damage they'd already inflicted."

"I'm sorry," I said. "It's awful."

She slid her hand over my kneecap, gave it a light squeeze with her manicured nails, then mercifully withdrew it. "I appreciate that." She rose off the bed and crossed slowly to the door and stopped. "You didn't know him at all, did you?"

"Don't reckon so," said Brooke. And I shook my head again.

"He went to Woodland's School, if you—"

"Nah, Graham. Nova did as well."

"I see."

"Anyway, he's older and that...I think. Probably."

"Hm." Suzanne turned and watched us for a moment. "It's just, ever since you came to see me, he's been unsettled."

"What do you mean?"

"I mean unsettled. He won't eat. He won't sit still. Keeps getting up and trying to leave. We've had to sedate him, just to get him to rest."

"You think that's our fault?"

"I'm just asking."

"Well, no, we don't know him. Not from school, not from work, not from anywhere...unless he liked to study your rogue's gallery file."

Suzanne glanced towards the window with the bird shit view. "It was so perfect, don't you think? After wasting years of my life, I finally got what I'd earned. What I deserved. This new world, it looks so good on me. Looks good on all of us."

"Yeah," said Brooke. "Just a shame seven and a half billion aren't around to see it."

Suzanne shot her a look, and then grinned. "I remember your mugshot, Brooke. Dead behind the eyes. Nothing there at all. But you're alive now. You're alive and living every moment. I can see it. You've never looked better."

"Oh, cheers."

"It's perfect for you now. Perfect for Nova. For my family. And it would be perfect for me too, were it not for that one little thing. That gnawing little concern."

"Yep. Must be a drag."

"Whoever broke my child, well, it would be lovely to meet them, one day. That's what I want. And if either of you happen to remember anything that might help me, don't keep it to yourself."

"Course not."

"I'd very much appreciate that."

Stevie moved aside and Suzanne backed out into the hallway. "I'll see you both in the morning."

Brooke listened at the door then barricaded it again while I heaved myself off the bed, retied the sheets and put them by the porthole. I also placed a hammer on the sill to break the glass if we have to. We didn't bother discussing how much she might've suspected us. It's academic now. Besides, another painful thought had hit.

"Man."

"Wot?"

"She said man. She knew."

Brooke sighed. Was she was losing patience with me? I wouldn't blame her if she was. "What are you talking about?"

"In the ballroom. I'm sure. We said about Alpamare. The murder. She...Suzanne...she said *man*. She said *man* when neither of us had specified."

"Really?" Brooke shuddered. "I missed that. But it's not exactly surprising, is it? Fucked up family."

It's nearly time. This might be the last entry. I keep thinking it will. If we get caught leaving tonight, I have no doubt that'll be it. The last sentence, the last word, and nothing but blank pages to the end.

18

Dear Brooke,

Where are you?

I've waited here for ages. I hope and pray you're alright. I'm heading out again to look. If...when you get here, just wait. I'll come back. If I'm not here by morning, then run, and don't stop running till you're far away.

If anything does happen to me, I need you to know that I don't blame you. We both decided on this. I wouldn't change anything, well...not when it comes to you and me. I learned to survive, but it was you who got me to live.

Your friend,

Nova xxx

19

Location: The Rendezvous – beneath Valley Bridge, the north end.
Time: Night.
Weather: Still.

Nothing. I traced my steps back along Westborough, checking as many buildings as I could, as well as the alleyways and bin stores. Still dangerous though, there's people everywhere. Running, crawling, lurking. The screams, they're all around. And the animals too. I keep picturing her lying injured somewhere. Bleeding out, with no one coming to help. Maybe I'm walking right past her, it's so hard in the dark, and I can't use the torch in case one of them sees. So worried.

It took forever for the sun to set. Once it had, we heard generators firing up and The Winner Takes It All began to blare. That was when we decided to make our move. Out of the door, along the corridors and down the stairs. We had planned to slip out the fire doors to the side, but the lobby was deserted and dark, and the front doors unlocked, so we crept that way. We didn't risk going back inside the ballroom to grab anything. Escape was the only thing on our minds. And escape is what we did. Right out the main doors, down the steps and into the street, where the air was cool and sweet. It was that simple. I was so sure we would be stopped, questioned, even dragged back up to our room and locked inside. But no. The few people we did pass barely glanced at us. I should've realised that was strange, but back then I still had some hope.

We ducked low, as we had done the day before, weaving through the cars, pausing occasionally to glance back to the hotel and see if anyone was watching. A few lights shone from the windows, but there was no movement. The entrance remained in darkness. Too easy.

Back in the flat, our belongings lay untouched behind the sofa. We gathered them up and made straight for the door. It was then we discovered our escape had been anything but. Running footsteps, echoing off the walls. A lot of them, drawing closer. Brooke rushed to the window, pressed her face against the pane and stared down. She turned back to me, her face pale.

"The family."

I joined her at the window. The crowd were moving up the road like an oil slick. I swear, I've not seen that many people since before the pandemic. Nowhere near. They were trying not to be loud, but there were so many of them it was impossible. Through the shadows I thought I could make out Suzanne at the front, flanked by her son and daughter. They knew where we were. They *had* been watching as we left, maybe just a few of them sneaking behind us, or even stationed in the surrounding buildings, observing as we passed below. It didn't matter how.

"They let us leave so they could hunt us," I said.

"It's cat and mouse," said Brooke. "But with a shit load of cats."

They bared down on our position, close enough now that I could see they were heavily armed: Bats, blades, hammers, a whole assortment of tools. I had visions of them dragging us out into the street. Beating, cutting, raping us. Maybe they'd douse our clothes in petrol and burn us alive like 17th Century witches. Panic rose in me.

"The back way," I said.

At the top of the staircase there was a narrow window which looked out over the backstreet. Torch beams danced through the air and dark figures snuck slowly along. They'd planned this well. We were surrounded. Why, why, why didn't we just leave?

Brooke threw off her rucksack and shoved it into my hands, the extra weight almost buckling my trembling legs. She drew the knife from her belt and wiped the blade on her arm.

"What…"

"It's a nice night for a run, don't you reckon?"

I just stared at her gormlessly.

"When it's all clear, or clear-ish, fucking run. Get to the rendezvous. Wait there for me."

"No, they'll kill—"

She pointed to the bags. "If that shit's weighing you down, toss it. We'll get more."

"Brooke—"

"There's no time. Just do it."

I grabbed her arm before she could descent the stairs. "You can't go out there."

She glared back at me. "It was my stupid idea to come to Scarborough. It was my stupid idea to stay, despite all the warnings. My idea to go in The Grand. All of it. I'm a dickhead. But I'll sort it, Star. I'll sort it." And before I could say another word, she had wrenched free of my grip and was bounding down the stairs, three at a time, before crashing through the front door.

Her voice sailed up. "GOOD EVENING, CUNTS."

Yells of excitement filled the air like jeers at a football match. Footsteps thundered past. I dropped the bags and rushed for the front door. It was flapping open and the backs of the crowd were bounding up the road. Not towards the centre but towards Falsgrave, where we'd been chased only yesterday. Where we'd almost died between lashing jaws. Brooke was out of sight, but I suddenly realised her plan.

She hadn't taken the knife out to fight them, she took it to slice through the rope that held the solicitor's door closed. The pack had been trapped inside for a night and a day - no food or water. They would've caught the scent of the crowd, long before they got there.

Suddenly, barks and screams filled the air. The family dispersed almost at once, flashes of glistening fur among them. Figures went down in the road, animals on their backs and at their necks. I could hear the tearing of cloth and flesh, and hear the ravenous snarls and the horrible cries of agony. Three people bolted right past me, the Great Dane snapping at their heels.

I slammed the door and flicked across the chain, then ran back up to the flat and locked myself in the bathroom, crouching on the brown tiles, waiting, my head against my knees, my hands pressing against my ears. I could still hear the sickening noise. I waited. I prayed that Brooke had managed to get away before the pack had pounced.

I waited.

At last the sound abated somewhat, and I picked myself off the floor and left the bathroom. I retrieved our bags. I checked through the front and back windows, then listened at the front door. I opened it, just a crack, and peered out. There was a man wailing but it was distant, as were the chorus of barks that followed. The street was clear. I slipped off the chain.

I jogged up towards Falsgrave Road and regretted it immediately. The broken rope swung gently from the doorknob like a dying snake. On the steps, pavement and road there must've been thirty bodies. Faces torn off, limbs gnawed, bones snapped. They were twitching. Groaning. Black blood stained the tarmac and trickled into the drains. Stevie, I think, lay on his back staring up at the sky, his chest cavity hollowed out.

I started to run, despite the weight of the bags. I was outside The Ship Inn before I realised I was going the wrong way. I turned back, went right down All Saints Road, then across the railway bridge and along to Valley Road. My lungs were burning, my heart thumping, the straps from the bags cut into my shoulders, but all that coursing adrenaline was keeping me upright. I hoped and hoped she would be waiting for me when I reached Valley Bridge, but there was so such luck.

I crouched in the shadows of the huge bridge support and tried to slow my thumping heart to a safe level. Above, the green paint was peeling and the metal beneath was red with rust. Years ago, tall, curved railings had been installed at either side of the bridge to stop people from jumping off, but that hadn't worked after the pandemic. Several flattened heaps lay close to where I was waiting.

As time dragged on, panic rose again like bile. Had she been among those torn up bodies in the road? Was she pinned down somewhere? Injured? Dying? Willing me to come help her. I couldn't bear it any longer. I wrote that note, left the bags here and retraced my steps. When I got back, there was nothing here but crushing disappointment. The diary was how I left it. Our equipment was untouched. I could've cried. I probably did. I'm so tired, but I'll never sleep. I can't even stay still. Come on Brooke. Please, come on.

Something awful has just occurred to me. What if she got caught and taken back to The Grand? Maybe she's there now, in that family suite, being questioned. Being tortured. Nailed to the wall and...oh god....

I've decided, I'm going there. I have to know. I'm prepped, I'm taking the Jar Jar bag with those few tools. I just have to know. One way or the other.

20

Time: Morning, I think.
Location: Under Valley Bridge.
Weather: Fog and smoke.

I can't see anything apart from my hand in front of my face. I don't know if this is a sea fret that's drifted in with the morning tide, or smog caused by the fire. Maybe a mixture of the two. Once upon a time there would've been the foghorn's mournful blast every thirty seconds, but it's silent now. After the deafening red night, everything's silent.

Yes, the fire. It burned on through the night and continued as I lay here in a fitful sleep. It makes sense I suppose. This diary began with fire, it seems fitting that it should end with it too.

The streets leading to The Grand were scattered with more chewed bodies than I cared to count. The dogs had clearly had their fill long ago, but the fleeing, screaming meat-bags proved too much to resist, so they carried on hunting and killing. I managed to stay out of their way. Only one close call, behind Pavillion Square, when a Bull Terrier approached the wheelie bin that I'd ducked behind. It clearly had the scent of something bigger and juicier, and scampered on without bothering me.

There was no one in the lobby of The Grand when I arrived, but I kept my knife at the ready just in case. I Have a Dream filled the air as I searched. I tried to listen for any movement, but couldn't hear much over the music, and occasionally, the drum of the generators. In the end, I lost all patience and began calling out for Brooke. Every floor, I cried out her name. I got nothing in return. She wasn't there. All I succeeded in was getting lost in the maze. It took ages to find the lobby again.

Mamma Mia echoed down. I hesitated at the top of the main staircase, trying to decide my next move. The rendezvous again? But if she was still alive, she might be bound and gagged somewhere. Was it worth breaking in a few more doors and shining my torch inside, just to be certain? How long did I have before the survivors (if there were any) returned to their home?

"NOOOVAAAa."

Ben jumped me from behind, just as he'd done last time. I managed to grab the banister and hold on for dear life before he could shove me over, but I lost my grip on the knife, and it clanged through the railings and stabbed, handle up, into the red carpet below. He was still strong, maybe stronger than before. Either that or I was weaker. His brown nails closed around my neck and he tried to force me to the ground. Struggling was useless, I had no energy left. I fought my way to the top of the stairs and let myself drop, and Ben dropped with me.

We rolled, entwined at first, then breaking apart. The floor and ceiling whirled and flashed as each step battered my flailing limbs. I landed heavily at the bottom and the breath was forced from my lungs. He tumbled on further and smacked headfirst against the rail and dropped like a sack of meat. I hoped he would just lay there, but of course, no. He rolled onto his stomach and crawled at me as if nothing had happened. I kicked out my legs and got several good hits on his arms and shoulders, but he barely flinched. And then he was on me. Over me. His face close to mine, his warm breath stinking like rotten cabbage. I realised then that our fall *had* damaged him. The spot where the family had desperately and crudely attempted to fix him up, was broken once more. His grey scalp had ripped open and was hanging off, and pieces of his skull were jutting out.

He pinned down my shoulders with his trembling claws. His face moved in closer. Warm saliva slobbered over my cheek. I clawed at his face and neck, but my efforts were wasted. He just wheezed out one word. "Frreeeeaassssshh."

Those remaining teeth were bared, and they closed slowly around the skin at my throat, not far from the scars he'd left before. There would be pain. Agony. Brooke wasn't here this time. Brooke was gone. But she'd certainly left her mark, I could see that now more than ever. That face, that skull: crumbling down the middle like the castle's keep. My nightmare come to life. But also, maybe, a chance...

I reached up with my right arm and gripped the edge of his wounded skull, feeling the slick, smooth bone at my fingertips. I touched the warm, fatty mass within and forced my nails through, then pulled and tugged, and a wet lump tore away in my hand, and I drew it out into the air.

His teeth were off my neck. The pressure on my shoulders had slackened. He'd straightened. He gurgled. His working left eye bulged like it might burst. His mouth twisted open - not like a scream though, it was a grin. A wide empty grin.

This time, I grinned back. "You like it fresh, Ben?"

I jammed the grey chunk of brain between his teeth and stabbed it to the back of his throat, managing to pull my fingers free as his mouth snapped shut and the stumps of his teeth crumbled. He gasped. Choked. And retched. His head jerked back and forth. His hands slid off me and closed around his swelling throat. I forced my hips up and to the side and he tumbled off and rolled against the stairs, still clutching his neck, his nails raking bloody tracks across it. His mouth opened and closed like a dying fish, his eye rolled slowly up into his head. One last, long wheeze and his arms fell to his side, and he lay still, staring through the cobwebs overhead.

I used the handrail to pull myself up and wiped my stained hand along the faded wallpaper, leaving a pinkish, grey smear.

"What have you done?" Alice was striding across the lobby, dishevelled, her jeans ripped and soiled. Her brown hair stuck to her sweat streaked brow. Behind her, an equally unkempt group looked on, glancing between Ben's lifeless corpse and me.

"Where's Brooke?"

"The bitch is dead," she snarled. "So are you."

I just shook my head. "You should've let us leave."

"Never."

I turned, stepped over Ben, and stumbled past the staircase and into the gloom of the passageway. Weary footsteps lurched behind me, and far away, Alice demanded that I stop. I passed the broken generator and continued deeper into the wave of choking fumes. I hadn't planned it. I just knew I couldn't outrun them. Not for long. When I reached the chained-up door, I'd already dragged the hammer from my bag. I slammed it into the glass panel, which broke on the third attempt. I reached for the matches...and you know that thing that happened in films and TV where the match never lit when they needed it to? That didn't happen. It sparked to life at once, and I flicked it through, seeing brief flashes of red plastic as it fell. I stumbled on, not knowing if it would do any good.

"BACK," someone screamed. And there was tremendous heat on the flesh of my arms.

"NO...GET HER."

I glanced around. A blinding flash. Yellow and blue flames curled the wallpaper and blackened the ceiling. Alice was tearing through, her eyes fixed on me, but her dress had already caught and crumpled, and she didn't notice until her hair was smoking too. She stopped to rip at her clothes and claw at her scalp, and then she vanished altogether among the dancing flames. I carried on, the air growing thicker, scraping my throat. There was a high roar, which grew louder with every step I made, drowning out every other sound, and then Thank You For The Music was silenced, permanently. I turned the corner, more passages. Smoke. Damp. Mould. Lost again. More stairs, concrete. Leading up. I remembered the way.

   I fell into the Empress Suite, and hurried through, knocking aside barstools and tables. The windows at the end had long been shattered and I jumped out and crossed the roof terrace, up to the railings. Much of the South Bay was masked by the night, but ahead the black sea crashed, and I felt cold splay brushing my cheeks. I could smell the smoke too, and hear crackling from close behind. The terrace was suddenly lit by a rippling streak of orange. I didn't turn. I leaned against the rails and looked over. A long drop, the ground in shadows, but there were thick white drainpipes that ran down the front. I didn't plan, I didn't think. Besides, a fatal fall would beat burning to death. I climbed over, I grabbed the nearest pipe and swung my legs off. The paint cracked apart in my fingers and against my chest as I jimmied down, but I ignored the scratching pain and kept my eyes forward, not thinking about the distance to the ground until my shoes finally made contact.

   I stumbled away, tripping off the curb and into Foreshore Road. The tide was high. A wall of water crashed over the promenade, and I tasted the salty spray and felt the icy droplets cooling my hot flesh. I spun right and ran, only looking back when the roundabout was in view, and I knew I was at a safe distance. What a sight. The South Bay, once illuminated by flashing bulbs and strobe lights, and slot machines and luminous neon signs, was now lit by an unrelenting red flame. The hotel's windows flickered, as every floor succumbed, and huge columns of black smoke dirtied the sky overhead. The crashing sea, as unrelenting as the fire, reflected the whole hideous scene.

21

Location: Home.
Time: Night/early hours.
Weather: The fog persists.

I came back and buried her. I buried them all. There wasn't a lot else to do. Not in the darkness and the fog.

I searched again for as long as I could, but with the walls of smoke and the distant growls – people or animals, I couldn't tell – it was just getting too hard, and there was another dusk drawing in. I couldn't face waiting at the rendezvous for yet another night, so instead I headed to Ramshill, and along to Filey Road. I didn't intend to come this far, but my legs, as weak and painful as they were, just kept on moving. Off to the right, through the grey shroud, I could see St Martins, my primary school. I remembered how every pancake day we'd finish at noon and troop down to the seafront, ropes in hand, to join in Skipping Day (an old tradition from the early 1900s when fishermen would give children old nets to skip with, while town labourers took a half day). Or how every Friday in assembly, we used to sing Scarborough Fair. I still remember all the words. They're playing in my head now. A droning accompaniment to my past that never seems to rest.

As Suzanne had confirmed, the family were yet to ransack this side of town. The majority of the parked vehicles were untouched, and the houses left undisturbed. Quiet tombs, including mine. It looks almost the same as when I left it, overgrown now of course. And smaller, much smaller.

Inside, there's more damp patches, and sprinklings of mould around the windows, and a few more cracks in the ceiling and some webs in the corners, but apart from that, it's how I left it. Frozen in time.

When did I last sleep? The Grand? When was that? I tried to distract myself by thumbing through the curled pages of my school history books, reading the various topics on Scarborough, but everything I saw was either a tragedy, or leading up to one. December 16th, 1914, two German battleships hit the town with five hundred shells, killing seventeen and injuring eighty more. WW2, the air raid, twenty-eight killed. The Civil War, 1645, hundreds died when half the keep was blown apart. Anne Bronte died here, aged just twenty-nine. James Paul Moody, born here, died at just twenty-four – he was the Sixth Officer on the Titanic. It goes on and on...

I couldn't sleep so I buried mum. Carefully wrapped her bones in the bedsheets, carried her out the back, dug a shallow grave in what was once her rose bed, and placed her remains into it. After that, I went over to Matthew's and buried him and his family. Still no rest despite all that digging through soil and mud, so I hiked to Westbourne Grove for Jenny. I've carved everyone's names onto stones from Mr Teal's rockery and laid them over each of their graves.

I've cried a bit. I never did before, I was too focused on the next move. But now I have the time, and the memories, and it all just poured out. I think I feel a bit better. Death is everywhere. I'm used to it, how could I not be. I've seen bodies almost every day for the past...however long. Thing is though, I'm not used to the idea, even now, that one of them won't pop their head around the door or call to me from the next room, or phone or text or email or tweet. They won't *like* or comment on my status updates or photos. They won't knock at the door or press the bell or peer in through the window. It won't happen, ever. I know that, but I never stopped expecting it. As much as I tried to. Perhaps now though, since I've finally laid them to rest, I'll stop anticipating it. Maybe now I'll just remember the good times (and yes, there were plenty, even with Ms Samara Edgecomb!) As for me, I'm not afraid to die - no more than I'm worried about going to sleep at night. To be honest, I'm not worried about much anymore.

The song in my head, keeps playing though...

Are you going to Scarborough Fair?
Parsley, sage, rosemary and thyme
Remember me to one who lives there
She was once a true love of mine.

Tell her to make me a...

My monkey mind settled and I finally slept. Just on the sofa in all my muddy clothes, but I was out of it for some time and there were no dreams. Not that I can recall, anyway. I must've cried some more because there are streaks through the grime under my eyes. The sun should be up soon. It might be up already, but it's so hard to tell in all the drifting grey. I'll go back to check under Valley Bridge first, and then decide from there.

Reminder: Go Belgrave – *I* went home, maybe Brooke had same idea.

22

Found her.

Busy.

Write later.

23

Time: No clue.
Location: Scarborough, duh.
Weather: Who cares!!

You're gonna fucking kill me when you see this!! But you're gagging to know everything what happened, but since you're fiiiiiiinally having a proper sleep, and my voice is still mostly fucked, then here you go...

It was a long shot with the dogs, I know that. They might've been asleep or had eaten each other already or escaped out of a window someplace. Anyhow, I ran to it and cut the rope and those arseholes were almost on top of me, but then the door swings open and it's like a hurricane of fur and teeth. 101 damnations!! They almost knocked me down, but I managed to duck and run. I didn't turn back, but all those screams...shit. I'm still hearing them.

People were still chasing me, not many but I could hear their steps behind mine. My legs were killing me, and my lungs felt like I'd breathed in a jar of curry powder. I'm coming up to Belgrave Terrace, so I go in there. I don't really think about it, I just do. Obvs, I'm used to the place, especially in the dark, so I reckon it made sense.

The front door's still open, I rush inside. It's pitch black, but I manage to avoid the furniture and all the shit on the floor. I don't know if I'm still being chased, but I keep on moving, into the lounge, maybe I'll head out the kitchen and out the back over the wall, while the chasers is still trying to find their way through.

But I trip, fucking Mark. Still a pain in my arse even after he's dead. I trip over his leg bone, and I fall on the stinking carpet. I'm going to get up again when my head explodes, and I fall back down like I'm drunk. Someone's stood over me. I reach for the knife, but the holsters empty. Probably dropped from my hand when I cut the rope.

"I know it was you, Brooke." Suzanne, her twatty voice panting hard and trembling with rage. "You hurt my boy."

Despite shitting my pants, I had to laugh. "Your *boy* was a sicko. I did you a favour."

BANG. My skull feels like a planet fell on it. I feel blood running over my neck.

"Suzie," I manage. "You should've heard his head crack. Like a rotten fucking egg."

She lets out an anguished growl, right, like one of those dogs. "I won't kill you, not completely. You're gonna know what it's like to be Ben. Damaged beyond repair. Then you'll get to know my family. Each and every one of them, again and again, until they're bored with you."

"Get stuffed."

"You won't be alone. You're little Nova will be right by your side."

Sounds corny, but it was when I heard your name, dude, that's when I got some extra strength. I tried to get up again, but the bat comes down across my back, and I'm sprawled out like a maggot on a hotplate. I desperately reach about. The floor's covered, there's gotta be something I can use.

She's raising the bat. I touch the TV remote. Some wires. A pair of headphones. Then denim. Then bone. Little bones. A withered foot, the one I bloody tripped on. Next to it, smooth plastic. A tube...thing. I remembered what it is.

The bat's above her head and she's taking aim. I lift the syringe, swing around and jab it into her shin and squeeze, emptying every last drop into her bloodstream.

Suzanne lets out a grunt and the bat comes down. I duck, but it hits my neck instead and I'm rolling over, panicking because I can't hardly breathe. I keep rolling until I hit the telly stand. I manage to get in a breath, but boy, that feels raw.

"What did you put...what is it?"

I hear a thump. It's nearby but, like, miles away, know what I mean? I can't move. Breathing is still hard and my head aches like a bitch. I think a hole has opened up and the house is falling into it. Before it goes dark, well *darker*, I think about you. I hope you make it out. I hope you don't wait too long for me at the rendezvous, but I'm fucked if I can remember where it is and even if I did, I aren't walking anywhere. I reach around, I touch bone again. It's Mark.

"Till death do us part, shithead."

When I wake up, I think I *am* dead and that. The room's red. It's kind of swimming around the walls. Suzanne's over by the couch, the needle still in her right shin. The drugs did their work. A lethal cocktail. There's rats on her. they've started to feast. I feel really gross, but I can't move any more. It hurts too much. I slowly turn away and look out the window.

The sky. That's where the glow is coming from. It's like a sunset, only not. Suddenly I know what it is. I know it was you what did it. I knew you'd be OK, cos you're like a proper survivor. Always have been, always will be. I'm glad.

Love you Star.

24

Time: Noon.
Location: Olivers Mount. WWII War memorial.
Weather: Wintery.

The leaves are almost down. The sea is a white foaming mass, but the tide's going out leaving a long stretch of slick sand dotted with strings of fragrant seaweed. There was a heavy frost first thing this morning, but that's thawed for the time being.

The view over Scarborough is amazing from up here (though not quite as good as the one from the castle's viewing platform on the curtain wall - where you can see the entire town without having to move your neck!) This was a test. Brooke insisted she was well enough to make it up here unaided, and she was right. I wasn't convinced at first, she seemed so much slower than before, but when we were halfway up and she broke into a rendition of I'm Still Standing, I realised she was going to be OK. It's such a relief, I can scarcely put it into words.

She was barely alive when I found her. At first, I didn't even recognise her. Just another corpse to add to the two already in the dingy lounge. If it hadn't been for the fox tattoo on her upper right arm (and the fact that the rats hadn't touched her yet), I might not have identified her at all. Her face and neck were severely bruised, and her right arm was dislocated at the shoulder. It was only when I put my ear to her mouth, did I hear her breathing: shallow and raspy.

"Brooke?" Her eyes had flickered a bit. "It's me."

She stared up blankly. "Stoopid trains. Can't you shut them the hell up?" My relief quickly dwindled.

"I'm Nova, a first aider. I just need—"

Her eyes were suddenly wide. "Star?" More growl than speech. "You have my mother fucking consent."

I snapped the arm back into place. I got the swelling down. I administered ibuprofen. The strikes to her head had been nasty, but I was relieved there was no fracture. When she next spoke, she said she wanted out of that "shithole" and shut down all my objections. "Please. It's doing me head in."

The mist had finally cleared when we left Mark and Suzanne for the final time. We must've looked bloody ridiculous heading down Filey Road, Brooke in a Tesco trolley, muttering deliriously, and me desperately trying not to lose control on the steep hills.

"Faster Chelsea," she mumbled. "Come on, faster. Move it. Before the cops get us?"

Back at home, I discarded the crusty, gross sheets and mattress from my old bed and made it into a kind of stretcher using cushions from the couch and armchairs. It was weird having her here. Laying where I had lay for most of my life. Two totally disparate parts of my world, suddenly collided. But it was fine. Her recovery was so much quicker here. She became more lucid with each passing day, pointing at my nerdy school photos and smiling, and even managing to thieve my diary a few nights ago (see previous entry), but I let her off. I was just glad she was able to.

So, this place was named after Oliver Cromwell, though no one knows if he actually visited it. It's hardly changed. The radio tower still stands. Olivers on the Mount Café is still intact, as is the obelisk shaped memorial, and apart from all the football pitches being overgrown, there's not a lot of difference. I remember when they used to have bike races up here every summer - made the whole town sound as if a massive swarm of bees were descending.

We can see for miles. The Grand is mostly gone, just two blackened walls remain. There's no sign of the family anymore. I've snuck into town several times for more bandages, etcetera, and seen no one. The survivors are either laying low or (as we suspect) have fled.

We cooked our tins of chilli with a camping stove I found in Kelly Shale's house, and as we slowly ate, Brooke turned to me, speaking with her mouthful.

"So what's the plan, Stan?"

"You think I always have a plan?"

"I don't think, I know! And I've passed the test haven't I? I've proved I'm not a total invalid, so when do we get going?" She picked up a crispy brown leaf off the ground and tossed it into the air. "The year's getting old."

I hesitated for a moment. I had no idea how she would take this. "I was wondering about staying on," I said at last. "Just for a while."

"Here?"

"Yes. A few months."

"Despite everything?"

"Yes. But I feel different now."

She nodded, clicked her tongue, and looked out across the town. "Hm."

"It's just an idea," I said. "Find some decent cover for the winter. Draw up a new list. Restock. Prep. Lay low. If you fancy tagging along for a while, you're more than welcome."

She laughed, almost spilling her bowl. "You know what, dude? Maybe I will. Possibly. For a bit at least. Till we're sick of each other."

25

Date: The Spring has sprung!
Location: The Spa.
Time: Dawn.
Weather: Mild.

~~Paracetamol, aspirin, ibuprofen, antihistamines, antibiotics, surgical blades, plasters, bandages. Tweezers.~~
~~Spare food.~~
~~Tin openers.~~
~~Spare changes of clothes.~~
~~Winter hats and gloves.~~
~~Spare masks.~~
~~Swiss Army Knives~~
~~Matches. Cigarette lighters. Candles.~~
~~Toothbrushes and toothpaste.~~
~~Tampons.~~
~~A hammer~~
~~A screwdriver.~~
~~Crowbar.~~
~~Sewing kit.~~
~~Two thermos flasks.~~
~~Two flasks for water.~~
~~Compass.~~
~~A length of rope.~~
~~Torches.~~
~~Spare batteries.~~
~~Toilet roll.~~

We're going soon.

  It's so much warmer now and the sky is clear. Last night we slept in The Spa, in a small storeroom behind Farrer's Bar. It's not that far from here where, in 1626, Thomasin Farrer discovered the spring water bubbling out of the cliffside and found that it had medicinal qualities (due in no small part to its high levels of magnesium sulphate.) Word spread and before long, thousands were flocking here to see for themselves, and that led to the construction of a simple wooden house, then a gothic saloon, and then The Spa Complex, with bars, a restaurant, a theatre, a sun court. The lot. The spring is long gone these days, but it's OK, Brooke and I are pretty well healed as of now!

Winter was harsh. We had gales, blizzards, snowdrifts, sea frets, you name it. We kept busy a lot of the time, which is why I haven't written in here for an age! I am happy (and relieved) to report that when the whiteouts did strike, we were ready. More than ready. We had set up a secure base in The Master Gunners House up on the castle headland. It's an 18th Century building with damp, drafts and a few crumbling stones, but those walls are bloody thick. Not surprising since they were constructed from broken chunks of the castle walls and keep. We managed to clear all the rubble from the south side chimney and trolley up a stack of logs from a cottage in the old town. When temperatures plummeted, we were able to warm our toes (and everything else) by a lovely crackling fire. Those nights were happy ones, even after a particularly rough storm left snowdrifts which kept us inside for several days. With nothing to do but read, play cards, eat through our decent quantity of supplies, sip warm mead from the bottles in the cellar, and then sleep some more…well, for the first time since that bolt of lightning found the roof of The Ravenhall, we were properly relaxed, and laughter was never far away.

During breaks in the weather, we set about the next phase of our future planning. The 'R' part of the ART of survival. Hunting, fishing, pouring through relevant books and learning to identity edible foliage and mushrooms and fungi, and healing herbs and minerals. We practiced lighting fires without matches, navigating without compasses and maps, building shelters, filtrating clean water to drink and growing vegetables. Also, a lot of first aid training (though as Brooke rightly pointed out, "We've had a shitload of that already!") It's early days, but we've made progress. I'm confident that when the day comes when the manmade food is no longer edible, we'll be ready. We'll be self-sufficient. Darwinners at long last!

There are others here. We began noticing signs of life after the last of the snow had thawed and we ventured down to the centre. Turns out, when The Grand burned and lit up the night sky, it was a signal to all the surrounding communities – a beacon like the one in the Roman era, only bigger, and not a warning this time. People who'd been driven out or scared away by Suzanne and the family, slowly but surely returned to their town. Dozens, maybe over a hundred. We kept our distance for a while, watching from afar, not engaging or leaving any trace of our presence here, but it soon became apparent that these were just folks trying to survive like us. We got to know a few of them, shared some stories and did a few trades. (Crates of mead and ginger wine in return for medical supplies.) Thank heavens, we were finally able to cross off the rest of our list. It felt good, them helping us, us helping them. It gave me hope.

If the human race is really in its final act, then it's reassuring to know there are still many good players on the stage.

Just stopped for a quick breather. We've reached the outskirts of town, or thereabouts. Back on the Cleveland Way, but the far side this time, heading south towards Filey. We'll be hiking inland soon, southwest, following the A165 for a time, and then...who knows. For once, we've not planned that far ahead. What we *do* know is that we'll be travelling further than before. A change of scene. New places. New horizons. Can't wait!

It's a little bit sad too though, watching the town slip out of sight behind the steep cliffs of Cayton Bay. I'll miss it, I really will. But then again, I suspect that at some point – maybe a year from now, maybe a decade – the North Sea will call us back and we will answer, and I won't be afraid - not even a little bit. Until that day, it's au revoir Scarborough, you windswept, salt-licked, sandy. spectacular, beautiful and historical lump of old England.

I'll leave it there. Brooke's waiting (giddy with excitement, of course), and time is getting on. We want to get as far along the road as possible before sundown. I've decided to let this go. Leave it on here. It certainly helped, even during those dark days, but I believe it has served its purpose now and I feel ready to begin a new chapter, so to speak. If you've found this and you've read it, I hope it passed a few hours – a long night watch perhaps, or a day indoors, squeltering from some adverse weather. I hope you're doing well and staying safe and feeling prepared for any challenges in the path ahead. Most importantly though, I hope, every day that you are living, *not* just surviving – that'll only get you so far.

Good luck and best wishes.

Your friend,

Nova.

Note from the author:

Thank you for reading. If you enjoyed No Longer Scarborough, please leave a rating on Amazon and/or Goodreads.

Special thanks to my family for your assistance, and to the people and businesses of Scarborough.

Printed in Great Britain
by Amazon